LIAR

WINIFRED MORRIS

LIAR

WALKER AND COMPANY

New York

First published in the United States of America in 1996 by Walker
Publishing Company, Inc.

Published simultaneously in Canada by Thomas Allen & Son Canada,
Limited, Markham, Ontario

Library of Congress Cataloging-in-Publication Data
Morris, Winifred.
Liar/Winifred Morris.
p. cm.
Summary: Fourteen-year-old Alex struggles to rise above the life
events which seem to conspire against him, from a mother who lies,
to a probation officer who won't give him a break, to bullies at his
new school.
ISBN 0-8027-8461-5 (hardcover)
[1. Mothers and sons—Fiction.] I. Title.
PZ7.M82923Li 1996
[Fic]—dc20   96-2465
CIP
AC

Book design by Jennifer Ann Daddio

Printed in the United States of America

2 4 6 8 10 9 7 5 3 1

In memory of Jerri DePriest, who helped me with the horse and hay-bucking scenes, and was always ready to share with me, and with so many people, her extraordinary warmth and strength

I didn't think Grandma would ever get the curtains just right. "I know the room is small," she said.

"It's fine," I said, and I was telling the truth.

Not that the truth had ever done me any good. People make a big deal about it, but it's the liars who win.

Still, with her fussing around like that, I figured I might as well tell her I really did like the room. It was tucked up under the eaves in the attic of the old farmhouse with the ceiling angled down. Yeah, I liked it. And I remembered it. It was one of the reasons I'd asked Ms. Lloyd if, maybe, I could come here.

Grandma straightened a rug I must've kicked. "I know Linda always liked this room."

Right. If my mom had liked this place so much, why hadn't she ever come back here? Why had I been here only once? Six years ago, when I was eight, I'd spent the summer here. But even then my mom hadn't come with me. She'd just put me on a bus with a name tag tacked to my shirt.

No wonder Grandma was nervous. She barely knew me. I barely knew her.

But this had to work.

I lifted my suitcase onto the bed and reached in my pocket for my knife. I needed to cut the duct tape that was holding the old suitcase together. I couldn't remember how many times I'd stuffed it full of my things.

I flipped open the knife. And Grandma jumped. Guess you couldn't blame her. I cut the tape, the suitcase fell open, T-shirts and jeans and paperback books spewed out onto the bed, and Grandma let out her breath.

She said, "I guess I should leave you alone to unpack. Supper'll be ready pretty soon."

Then, just as she was going out the door, she turned and added, "Alex, I want you to know how glad we are to have you here. We're both glad to have you here. I know your grandfather seems gruff, but . . ."

"It's fine," I said again. Grandpa hadn't said two words to me all the way here from the bus station, the three of us wedged in the cab of the pickup truck, but that was just fine with me.

Grandma said, "I wanted you to know. That's just the way he is. Please don't think you're imposing on us in any way. We were both glad to have you come here. We both want you to be happy here."

Then, finally, she was gone.

And it felt good to be left alone. Not locked up

alone in a puke green cell with a stainless steel john. Just alone for a minute, to think.

How had the stakes gotten so high? Sure, the cops liked to threaten you. But the juvenile court, all they ever did was talk to you. Then send you home.

Until now.

I reached into the pile of clothes and pulled out the dog-eared books. For a moment I just looked at them—these books I'd been hauling around for years—and felt how much I wished I could be like the guys you saw on the covers, their hats pulled down to shade their eyes, their rifles lying easy across their saddles. You could tell they'd never get themselves in a mess like this.

I stacked the books on top of the dresser, and I let myself slip into the dream. Which was easy to do, standing there, 'cause the window above the dresser looked out on a world just like the covers of those books. It was easy to imagine myself riding up the valley I saw, up toward the mountain I saw whitish blue in the distance.

You couldn't see another house out that window. On the drive from the bus station, I'd been surprised at how few people lived out here. We'd pass a house, then there wouldn't be another until a mile or more down the road.

I'd been surprised by it, but I'd also remembered it. This place so much like the dream. No wonder I'd thought of it when Driscoll, my probation officer, and Ms. Lloyd, the social worker, and Judge Robbins were

all coming up with their ideas of what to do with me.
After all, you were supposed to be able to ask your
grandparents for things.

But the men in my books, they never asked anything of anyone. I wanted to be like that too.

Then Grandma was calling up the stairs.
"Supper."

"OK," I called back, and I started stuffing my
clothes into the drawers of the dresser, which were
empty. Grandma must've cleaned them out for me.

So why hadn't she cleaned out the whole room?

All I could see now were my mom's old stuffed
animals. Some mice in frilly dresses, a huge pink giraffe,
and cats and bears and monkeys and stuff, all lined up
across the headboard of the bed. As if she still lived
here. The comfort of the dream was gone. I could smell
her in the room.

I sank down onto the bed. I took down the pink
giraffe and leaned back against the headboard holding
that giraffe tight against me, just like a little kid. I could
feel it soft against my cheek, but the wood of the headboard was hard. It hurt where it pressed against my
shoulders and my head. I felt that too. But I couldn't
move.

I was glad no one could see me like that, hugging
a dumb stuffed animal. I was thinking that as if one half
of my brain was seeing things from somewhere else.
Somewhere rational.

But with some other part of my mind, the part that is always screwing up, I pulled my knife from my pocket. I pressed the point into and through the pink fur, right into the long pink neck. "You've got to learn to manage your anger." I could almost hear Ms. Lloyd saying that to me, as I watched the white stuffing swell out behind the blade.

I'd started the dream so long ago I couldn't remember not having it. Back when my mom was so much bigger than me there really wasn't anything else I could do, I must've seen a TV Western. Then, whenever I needed it, I'd have this dream. I'd see myself riding off into the sunset. Getting away from the bad guys. The dream would let me find sleep.

But that night I couldn't see myself riding off anywhere. Instead, I kept seeing that stuffing all over the bed. And Grandpa watching me pick up every piece of it. With Grandma running in and out of the room, her arms full of stuffed animals. Storing them away somewhere else. Rescuing them from me.

"Just one false move," was what Driscoll had said. He'd never been in favor of letting me come here. Would they call him and tell him I'd blown it already? And he could come take me away to MacBride, the "training school" he'd guaranteed would straighten me right out.

But in the morning Grandma called up the stairs without saying anything about Driscoll or MacBride, just that it was time to get up. And when I got down to the kitchen, I found her scooping pancakes onto a plate. There was also warm maple syrup. And her homemade butter I remembered from that summer I'd stayed here. It was round and sat in a little blue and white bowl in the center of the table.

Would anyone fix a breakfast like that for some- one they were going to send away?

But it wasn't until I was carrying my dishes to the sink, trying to do everything right—so why had I stabbed that stupid giraffe?—and Grandma said, "They're going to start sending the bus up here, but I'll drive you to school today," that I knew for sure I was getting another chance.

Outside the grass was flecked with white. It crunched under my feet. I could see my breath as I waited for Grandma to back the pickup out of the garage. I rubbed my hands together, bounced from foot to foot, and thought about how it had been so hot here that summer you had to jump in the pond in the middle of the day. But now it was October, almost November. My mom had told me about it snowing so much they had to close the schools, and how she used to build these big snow forts. I'd never lived anywhere where it got cold like that.

But pretty soon I was in the truck with the

heater cranked up, and we were bouncing back down the gravel road we'd come up the day before. Going past the same empty hills, until we reached the town of Rimrock.

I hadn't seen Rimrock before. Maybe back when I was eight, but not the day before. We'd just driven past a sign that said "Rimrock 1 mile." Now when I saw it, I liked it. It had one street, one gas station, and a row of stores that must've been there since pioneer times. It was the closest thing to an old west town I'd ever seen.

But the school didn't look like the town. Instead it looked like a lot of the new schools do, only smaller. No windows, like a prison. I wasn't surprised. When you're always the new kid, you can't expect school to fit into your dream.

"I'll park," said Grandma, "and go in with you."

"No, I can do it," I said, and when she had to stop in the line of cars pulling into the lot, I jumped out, didn't give her a chance to argue or catch up with me.

I made my way through the bikes and the book bags thrown on the ground and tried to figure just how bad this school thing was going to be. There were a bunch of little kids. Which was weird. Why was I going to the same school they went to? At least there were some my age too—three or four groups of them standing around. But even they didn't look much like what I was used to.

The guys all had hair so short you could see their scalp. And they all wore baseball caps, and flannel shirts like lumberjacks. *Red* shirts and baseball caps. While for years I'd made a point of not wearing anything brighter than gray.

I had to go here. I had no choice. "Regular school attendance." It was one of the things Driscoll had put on the "terms of probation" list. But looking at these guys looking at me made me think of the other big thing Driscoll had put on that list.

There's always one guy in every school who's going to make you miserable until you take him on. You just have to face up to that. He's probably nastier than you, so more than likely you'll lose. Still, if you put in any kind of showing at all, it'll get you respect.

But just about the biggest thing on Driscoll's list was "no fights."

Maybe I should've gone along with Ms. Lloyd's idea of cutting my hair. I pulled open one of the wide double doors, thinking there was nothing I could do about that now, and just inside I was stopped by a man with thin graying hair, who still looked like he could take on any of the kids sizing me up outside. He said, "Alex Shafer." It wasn't a question. "I'm the principal here. Hodson," and he offered one of those handshakes that lets you know who's in command.

Still, he seemed OK, just your standard principal, and I thought I could handle this part of the school. The adults, the lectures, the rules. Lately I'd been getting plenty of practice with that sort of thing.

Then he said, "No doubt about it. I can see your dad in you."

And I felt like someone had hit me from out of some blind spot, from out of some place I never would've thought to look.

"You play football?" he asked.

I managed to say, "Not really."

"Too bad. Your dad was the best we ever had. The colleges were all bidding for him. Your mom must have told you that."

"No." It came out more of a cough than a word. All my mom had told me about my dad was that he'd got her pregnant when she was seventeen, then left when I was two. She'd called him lots of things, but never a football hero.

"Bruce had real talent."

Even the name sounded strange. My mom never called him Bruce. The nicest thing she called him was "your dad," and even then she made it sound like she was swearing.

"Bruce was always a favorite of mine. I was the coach back then. Course he was young and in love. Can't talk sense into a kid who's in love. Believe me, I tried. He just walked away from all those scholarships." Then you could tell he'd quit seeing good old Bruce in me. "But from what I hear, you're not much like him. I want you to know this is a clean country school. We don't need problems like you. Give me a reason, anything, and I'll have you out of here so fast it'll make your head spin."

My head was spinning already.

He kind of jerked his chin like he was pointing with it. "McCauley's the person you need to see. Our counselor. His office is over there."

3

I stumbled down the hall to the counselor's office, thinking of these fuzzy, very old, and kind of scary memories of my mom and me hurrying out of town because my dad was after us. And wanted to hurt us somehow. At least that's how it had felt.

It had been a long time since my mom had blamed our moves on him. Now I knew she got checks from him. Waiting for his checks, counting on his checks, had become a big deal each month. But I guess I still thought of him that way, when I thought of him at all, as this guy we had to run from in the night.

Even though I now knew how much my mom lied.

She was really good at lying. Skilled. She could say anything, and you'd believe her. She'd look the landlord right in the eye and say, "I paid the rent. I put the money in an envelope and slid it under your door. Don't tell me you didn't find it!" The poor landlord would come to think there might've been an envelope on the floor, and he'd somehow missed it. Maybe he'd kicked it back out the door. And it wasn't a check, my mom would insist. "It was cash.

All the cash I had. You mean somebody took it!"
Sometimes we could go for months without paying the
rent.

But even though I could understand her telling lies
like that, and I'd sometimes be in on them with her, laugh-
ing at how dumb some people were, it had taken me a long
time to see she lied to me too.

Yeah, she was very good. Driscoll had sure believed
her.

No one was in the counselor's office. I let myself in.
And there was my file lying open on his desk. I shuffled
through the papers, half curious, but the words blurred in
front of my eyes.

It had been easy to believe my dad had been like her
usuals, but that Hodson guy hadn't thought my dad was a
sleazeball. A favorite of his? I couldn't imagine any of my
mom's boyfriends being anybody's favorite.

I gave up on trying to read that stuff.

What if my dad had wanted me back? And that was
why he'd chased us—if he'd really chased us—if anything
she'd told me was true.

I decided to show them what I thought of their file,
and this whole mess she'd put me in. Except I didn't have
any matches on me. But there had to be something here
that would work. I found a lighter in a drawer, probably
confiscated from some kid. I flicked it open and watched
the flame leap up.

Then a man walked in, and I stopped. Stopped

everything, stopped breathing. I stood there, frozen, bent over the desk, holding the flaming lighter just above the open drawer.

The man had curly blond hair that stuck out every which way. He said, "I see you found my office, Alex," and held out his hand.

So I closed the lighter and dropped it back into the drawer. Shook the guy's hand, pulled away, then sank down into a chair.

The man sat down too and pushed the drawer shut. "Well, you really know how to start things off right."

There was nothing I could say to that. At least he'd come in when he did, before all those papers went up in flame. Would he pick up the phone and call Driscoll right now? Why did I do these things? I could almost see the handcuffs on my wrists.

"You know, we don't get too many kids like you." Right, this is a clean country school. "Usually all I do is help the kids get classes they like." My hands were shaking; I sat on them and willed them to stop. "I'd like to do more for you. You can't keep on hitting out at things. Or setting fire to them. Fortunately, you didn't do that." So maybe he wouldn't call Driscoll. "The point is, you've got to make some changes, but I'm not sure how I can help. I really don't know much about you. I have your school records, of course," and he glanced down at the file, "but not much from the juvenile court."

That got my attention. I thought they would've told him everything.

"So I hope you'll tell me a little about yourself. Maybe not the big stuff. Not now. But maybe you could tell me what you like to do. I don't see any sports in these records. Because of your grades, I guess, and moving so much. But there must be something you like to do."

My hands had quit shaking. What he was saying was finally sinking in. He really didn't know everything. I realized I might be able to get him on my side, in spite of the thing with the lighter, the way I'd gotten Ms. Lloyd on my side. It pays to have someone on your side.

So I decided to answer his question, and give him the answer you could count on working with school people. I said, "I like to read."

"Really? What do you like to read?"

"Westerns, mostly."

"Then you like this kind of country."

"Yeah, I guess."

"It's nice country, all right. I like it too. I like the way it smells."

I thought that was a weird thing to say, but somehow it made me think of the smells I remembered from here. Six-year-old smells, but I found them coming back. The pond, the pine trees, the hay in the barn.

"Still, you've spent most of your life in cities. Have you thought about the things you're going to miss out here?"

"Yeah." And the kids were sure different.

But I'd asked to come here. And not just because my other choice was MacBride.

I felt that now, just how much I wanted to make it here. Maybe because I was still remembering those old smells. I felt how much I wanted things to be the way they'd been that summer. And stop being the way they'd been all the rest of my life. The feeling came on so strong, I had to turn away to keep from showing too much.

"Well, I hope it works out for you. By the way, you can call me Jake."

That sounded like he was winding things up. Which was good. I sure wasn't interested in a long conversation.

But it turned out, just like that Hodson, he had some trick moves.

"One good thing about you coming here, now you'll be able to spend more time with your dad."

He said that, and I lost it. I looked at him with all my confusion showing, I knew. I couldn't hold this in.

He said, "I thought . . ." You could see he was confused too. "I guess I assumed. I really wish they'd filled me in on you better. I'm sorry."

I said, "He lives here?"

"Really, I thought you knew. The laws that protect a juvenile's privacy can be frustrating at times. The grapevine has told me more about you than Mr. Driscoll has. I just assumed Bruce had been paying child support and seeing you once in a while. And now would be able to see you more."

I said, "No," even though it was true about the child support.

"Well, regardless of how Bruce plans to handle this, I think you have the right to know. He lives a little north of town. He's married again, and he and his wife have three kids."

4

My mom must've known. All those checks must've had return addresses on them.

She'd acted like my dad was always on the move. Like us. Or maybe back in San Jose, where he'd left us — stalked out one night, according to her — when he'd been here long enough to have three more kids!

Why had she lied about that?

It was all I could do to find the room I was supposed to go to. But I knew I'd better get this stuff out of my head. Later, I told myself, or you won't make it through the day.

Somehow I survived until lunch. When I was glad to see everyone even close to my age jump into a pickup truck and roar off somewhere. But that left me in the lunchroom with a bunch of screaming kids who didn't look older than ten. Knowing some of them might be my half-brothers or half-sisters didn't help. I sat at the end of a long metal table, pressed up against the wall, with kids slurping milk all around me, squeezing ketchup into their applesauce, and tossing tater tots at each other, and I waited for the bell to ring again. To rescue me from that hell and send me to another.

Sophomore English. *Romeo and Juliet.* The teacher was a woman with large round glasses and a full skirt that bounced out from her waist kind of like a parachute and hung nearly to the floor. It looked like she might not have any feet and was floating around on that skirt.

"Alex, maybe you've read this already."

Oh, sure, I always read this kind of stuff. "No, ma'am," I said.

She said, "We're in Act Two, scene four. You can be Mercutio."

"Wrong. Mercutio is a guy. She should be Juliet." This from a kid named Wyatt. With each bell I moved to another room, but it was always the same kids. Sometimes one or two of them changed, but this one, Wyatt, I'd come to know well. He hadn't let up once about my hair, or the earring I'd also insisted on keeping.

The guy was big—big neck, big shoulders and thighs—but whenever he said anything, he always looked over at another kid, Trevor. Already I knew you didn't do anything in this school without Trevor's OK. At least not in the sophomore class. He was one of those movie star–looking kids who seemed born to rule.

Now he laughed his approval and added to the joke. "The new girl? Naw, she's too ugly for Juliet. There must be a better part for her. How about those witches with the cauldron?"

"Wrong play," said a girl who sat across the aisle from me. She said this without even looking up from whatever it was she was drawing. A horse, I thought, but a funny-looking horse. It looked like it was playing a guitar.

The teacher said, "Now, boys."

I just scrunched down further in my seat. Which wasn't my usual way of handling this sort of thing.

"Make Wyatt read," said the girl.

But the teacher, who had floated over to the other side of the room, asked another kid, a scrawny redhead she called Barry, to read the other part. And the two of us began the chore of stumbling our way down the page.

While the rest of the class imagined what fun it was going to be when Wyatt and me got it on.

But that's not going to happen, I told myself. You've already screwed up enough.

And I did make it through the day. Then I managed to get my locker open one more time, after rattling the lock, yanking on it, and rattling it again. I stuffed all the books I'd been given into the locker and slammed the door shut. If I'd been given homework to do, I couldn't remember what it was. And I didn't care. I just wanted out. Fortunately, the crowd was all moving in the direction I wanted to go, and soon I was outside.

But there was a whole row of school buses parked at the curb. Which one was mine?

"You want number three," said a voice behind me. I turned. It was that McCauley guy, Call me Jake.

He said, "How'd it go?"

"OK."

He smiled, like I'd made a joke.

Then I was heading for the bus. But that counselor and his knowing smile had made me think of the lighter and Driscoll, and that principal who had been my dad's coach. Things I'd been deliberately keeping out of my head. I was remembering my dad was here! He might be waiting in one of these cars to pick up his kids. His other kids.

Did he know I was here?

I wasn't looking where I was going. And Trevor and Wyatt were suddenly in my way. They were dressed in their football gear, carrying their helmets, and Wyatt blocked me, sent me stumbling backwards.

"This new girl is sure clumsy," he said.

I managed to stay on my feet, regained my balance, and faced him, ready, fists up. Wyatt grinned at me. We both knew Jake was watching.

"Hey, maybe you need glasses," I said, which was lame but the best I could come up with right then. At least I stood him off long enough to make it clear I wasn't backing down. Then we sidled past each other, almost but not quite grazing shoulders. Three more steps and I was jumping on the bus.

Where I collapsed into a seat. Glad to see there were no other boys my age on the bus. It looked like all the high school boys went to football practice after school. I could see them gathering out on the field. Even that scrawny little redhead Barry was out there, his football jersey hanging to his knees.

Here they must need every guy in order to fill out the team. And still probably never won.

Except when my dad had played.

I rode back down those gravel roads, getting farther and farther away from the school, and when I got back to my grandparents' place, I found the cold of the morning was gone. I could feel the sun on my back as I walked up the drive to the house, and there was the mountain in front of me again.

Then I opened the door and was met by the smell of fresh chocolate chip cookies, bringing back what that Jake guy had said. Bringing that terrific summer back too. Grandma poured me a glass of milk — "Thought you might be hungry" — and I found myself sliding into the scene. As if maybe all those years in between had never happened, and I'd always come home to cookies and milk.

Instead of my mom passed out on the couch. Or there with her latest boyfriend. "When you're supposed to come home, you never do. Then when I want a little time alone, you have to show up, of course."

The cookies were so warm the chocolate chips were still soft. They made all that stuff about my mom, and also the day at school, even what I'd learned about my dad, fade the way nightmares do when the sun comes up. There was just Grandma's great cookies. I dunked one in my milk.

Then Grandma said, "You'll need to change your clothes."

Between mouthfuls I asked her why.

"Your grandpa wants your help out at the hay shed. He's already out there waiting for you. Do you have some clothes you can work in?"

The cookie in my mouth went dry.

Sure, I'd known Grandpa would want me to work. Even back when I was only eight, Grandma and Grandpa had both made it clear farm kids worked. I'd fed the chickens, gathered the eggs, put fresh straw in their nests. By the end of the summer, I'd gotten pretty good at milking the cow. But things had been different with Grandpa this time. Even before the giraffe. You really couldn't expect him to be too pleased with me now.

But I put on some jeans with a hole in the knee. Grandma gave me one of Grandpa's old shirts, after making a big deal about how tall I'd gotten—well, what did she expect? Then I went out to the hay shed, much as I didn't want to.

Grandpa had backed the old flatbed farm truck up to the shed, and he was standing on top of the stack of hay. He called to me, "Climb up here." I couldn't tell by the way he said it if he was still mad about the giraffe, or just mad at me in general, or what. But there was nothing for me to do but climb up to where he was.

There he handed me some things that looked like Captain Hook's hand. Except there were two of them. He said, "Work the bales on down to the truck. And don't throw 'em. I don't want to get hit in the head with one."

He was a tall, skinny, old guy. Built kind of like me, I guess. Bald, and he refused to wear a hat, so his head was browned by the sun. Now I watched him make his way down to the truck. The bales were like huge stair steps. He jumped across to the bed of the truck, then yelled, "What you waitin' for?"

So I put down the hooks.

I tried to pick up a bale of hay. I grabbed it by the wires that were wrapped around it and only managed to hurt my hands. "City kid," Grandpa yelled at me. "Look." He held up two hooks like the ones he'd given me. Holding them by their wooden handles, he reached around the ends of a bale and lifted. "Get it?"

"Right." I picked up the hooks and tried again. "Hey, what do these things weigh?"

"'Bout ninety pounds," came the reply. "Some guys make 'em heavier. But that don't make no sense to me unless you're payin' by the bale. I figure I have to lift 'em myself, so I bale 'em light."

Light? I figured more than likely he *was* mad at me.

But it was hard to tell. I started to carry the bale down to the truck and stumbled, and Grandpa yelled up at me, "You don't have to work that hard. Gravity's on your side." So maybe he wasn't mad after all. I found it sure was easier to tip the bale down onto the next step instead of picking it up. Gravity *was* on my side. Then it was easy to shift it down one more step, and one step at a time, pulling with the hooks, I worked it down to the truck.

There Grandpa took it to the front of the bed, but all he said was, "Now, you don't have to watch. Get on up there and get another one."

So I hustled back up the stack of hay, got the next one in the row, and worked it down to the truck the same way. This time he said, "You know, we're just gettin' older out here."

The old man's voice was flat and easy—he didn't sound mad—but my mom had always complained about him, said you just couldn't please him. Maybe on this one thing she'd been telling the truth. I brought down another bale, and he said, "You'd think a boy your age could move faster than that."

I thought about just dropping the hooks and going back into the house. I had to remind myself how much I wanted to be here.

So the next time I let gravity do even more of the work. But then the bale started moving too quickly, picking up momentum. I remembered what he'd said about not wanting to get hit in the head. I grabbed for it with one of the hooks and felt my arm being yanked half out of its socket before I got the thing to stop. But this time Grandpa said, "Now you're beginnin' to get the hang of it."

Still, he was sitting on one of the bales, making it

really obvious just how bored and well rested he was by the time I got there. Of course, he was going to be done first. All he had to do was put the bale where he wanted it on the truck. Even though he seemed to be pretty particular about that, arranging the bales kind of the way kids build with Lego blocks, I felt I was doing ten times the work, as I ran up and down that stack of hay.

I had to take off the shirt. Then the hay scratched my arms and made them itch. My hair kept falling down into my eyes. It was wet. I kept brushing it back. Then I had hay and dirt in my eyes, and I was still running up and down that stack of hay. My arms began to ache. I was getting dizzy. But each time I got to the truck, Grandpa'd be looking as fresh as ever. And often he'd say something like, "It would've been easier to take that other one first." Well, all right, I hadn't seen that it would've been easier to get the bales in a little different order, but why hadn't he said something about it before? Like it was all very funny to make me work harder than I had to.

But the pile was getting lower. The run to the top was getting shorter. Then I wasn't having to go up at all, just bringing the bales straight across, and Grandpa was stacking them onto the very back of the truck.

"I think that'll do 'er," he said. "Bet you're thirsty," and he tossed me a two-liter pop bottle. I twisted off the cap, tipped it up, and found it wasn't pop at all, just plain old water, something I never drank, but it sure tasted good.

I swigged down some more of it, then looked back

and saw I'd leveled one whole row. Also I'd shown the old guy I could take what he was dishing out.

But then he said, "City kid," again. "You'd think you'd been workin' all day. Bet you figure it's time to go in and rest." Yeah, I'd been thinking that. "Put on your shirt and get in the truck."

But he walked to the passenger side of the truck. I watched as he climbed in on that side.

"Quit nursin' that bottle," he said.

So I grabbed the shirt and jumped down off the hay, but I was confused. Maybe this was some kind of foreign truck with the steering wheel on the right-hand side, except I knew it was a Dodge. I walked over to the other door, looked in the window, across the steering wheel that was just where most steering wheels are, and said, "You want *me* to drive?"

"Sure. Why should I do everything?" I decided he didn't know how old I was, but he said, "Aren't you almost fifteen?" Then maybe he didn't know how old you had to be to drive. But I wasn't about to argue when he said, "Come on. We haven't got all day."

"Haven't you driven at all?" he asked as I climbed up into the driver's seat.

"Well, a little." One time I'd driven my mom's car, out of the garage and then into the garage and then out of the garage again. I'd just been practicing, but she'd caught me and thought I was trying to steal it or something. I didn't explain all that. I just said, "It was an automatic."

So Grandpa explained the clutch and the gears. And I listened really close. Suddenly I wasn't dizzy at all. Or tired. I'd forgotten all about wanting to go in the house. I moved the shifter through the gears a few times with the truck not running. Then I found the brake with my foot. Found the gas, too, then the brake, then the gas. It all felt really good.

"Now you might as well start 'er up," said Grandpa. "Life is just gettin' shorter out here."

I did everything exactly the way he told me. The engine roared, then settled down. Slowly I let out the clutch, and then . . .

"A little more gas next time."

Again the engine roared, and kept on roaring. "Not that much. You're gonna blow 'er up! There. Now ease off the clutch."

And we were moving!

"Now turn to the left, not fast, but start turnin', more than that. Come on, Alex, we don't want to run into that gas tank there. OK, now straighten 'er out. See that road between them fences? Think you can make it? Or think you're gonna take out the fence?"

I was concentrating more than I thought I ever had. Then I was passing between the two fences. And the road was straight. Now that I was on it, I heard myself take a deep breath. It might've been the first breath I'd taken since starting the truck.

"Well, that's a relief. I sure didn't want to put in a

new fence. Now we're just gonna go on out to the end of this road. See them cows out there? Well, that's where we're goin'. Straight on out this road. So you can go a little faster. Them cows are hungry, you know. Now, when you hear the engine doin' like that, you should shift into second gear."

Then Grandpa pulled a can of tobacco out of the glove box. He took a paper out of the can, cupped it between his fingers, and began to roll a cigarette. He didn't say another word to me, didn't tell me I was doing a good job or anything, but he wasn't paying any attention to the road. And I kept the truck between the two fences, aimed it right down the gravel track, until I came to a wooden gate.

Grandpa had just been relaxing with his cigarette, looking out at the scenery it seemed, but he said, "Now, you're not gonna drive through that gate, are you?" I shoved the brake to the floor. The truck lurched to a halt. And the engine died. "Next time put in the clutch."

The road had been taking us up the valley toward the mountain, and on the other side of the gate, the forest began. But here it was still open fields. On one side green, on the other side brown.

I was looking at the green one when Grandpa said, "The new wheat. It ain't doin' so good. One of the driest years we've had. Nothin' we can do about that. But we're goin' in the stubble there, where the cows are. Think you can open that gate?"

The only gate I saw was the wooden one. "Where the cows are," Grandpa said. Then I saw what he meant. It wasn't much of a gate, just a stretch of barbed wire that was separate. I got out and started wrestling with it, and Grandpa shouted, "They don't teach you anything in the city, do they."

Finally I figured out I was wrestling with the wrong end. You'd think he could've told me. And all the time I was tossing slabs of hay to the cows, with him driving slowly through the field, he kept yelling stuff like that at me, telling me how stupid I was. Like I was supposed to know how much hay a cow likes to eat.

But he had me drive the truck back to the house, and even into the shed. And that time when I put on the brakes, I put in the clutch too.

Then at the dinner table that night, he said, "He didn't do too bad." And as I scooped on another helping of mashed potatoes and poured on enough gravy that it flooded everything else on the plate, the pot roast, the biscuits oozing with butter, even the green beans—which had big hunks of bacon poking out of them—I felt better than I could remember ever feeling before.

I felt so good I almost asked about my dad. Had they talked to him? Would he come see me? But each time I tried, nothing came out. And they didn't mention him.

That night I fell asleep so quick I didn't need the dream at all. But the next morning I crawled out of bed so stiff I could hardly move. "City kid," Grandpa said. "You do a little work with him, and the next day he walks like a crab." Still, I decided he was just gruff, the way Grandma had said. He seemed to actually like me.

In the shower my shoulders and back loosened up. It felt so good, I stayed there so long, I hardly had time to eat. But it was bacon and eggs, fresh eggs from Grandma's chickens, with these big dark orange yolks, and a pile of potatoes too, so I managed to shovel it down and thought a guy could get used to this kind of stuff.

Then Grandma was telling me she could see the bus. So I grabbed the pack she'd given me to carry my books—as if I was going to bring home books—and went out to catch it.

Hardly anyone was on the bus. Guess I was near the end of the line. But the football team wouldn't have practice in the morning, so I picked my seat carefully. I didn't go all the way to the back. That was always staked out by whoever was in power on the bus. I went halfway back — that was usually neutral territory — purposely dropped my empty pack in the seat beside me, then stretched out my legs, leaned back, and tried to look asleep.

The bus bounced up and down the gravel roads lurching to stop after stop. At each stop more kids got on, but most of them were younger than me. Some were so tiny they waited for the bus holding their moms' hands. They looked like red and blue marshmallows in their jackets that were all too big. Kids that were a little older than that roughhoused down the aisle, and the driver would yell at them to get to their seats and stay in their seats. I watched all this action through the haze of my eyelashes.

And I thought about my dad's kids. At least one had to be old enough to go to the school. But Jake had said he lived north of town, so his kids wouldn't be on this bus.

Neither Trevor nor Wyatt got on. They must've ridden another bus too, or managed to get a ride. Not very many high school kids got on. I knew as many as could wouldn't ride the bus. It was never cool to ride the bus.

The girl who'd been drawing the funny-looking horse got on and said hi as she went by. Other than her, no one talked to me. My sleeping act was working pretty good.

Then the red-headed kid, Barry, got on. By then the bus was pretty full. Still, I was surprised when he slid in next to me.

"Mind if I put your pack on the floor?"

I looked at him. He was friendly enough, or he would've thrown my pack on the floor. Or out the window.

"Is it OK?" he asked.

"Sure, I guess."

"Where you from?"

The last place I'd lived was Portland—my official place of residence, according to the juvenile court— but I'd been there only three months. There were at least twenty cities, from four different states, that would've answered his question. I decided on L.A. only because everyone knows where it is.

Barry was impressed. "Really? That's gotta be better than here. I been to Disneyland." Then he stared at the floor, which didn't make any sense. Until he said, "At least we were going to go. But the woods was shut down early that year. And my dad hurt his back." He looked back up at me. "You been to Disneyland?"

"Sure."

"What's your favorite ride?"

"Space Mountain."

"Right. I've heard about that one. I'm going to go

on it first." He took another minute to stare at the floor. Then, reviving again, "L.A., that'd sure be a great place to live. You meet any movie stars?"

Now I realized I'd seen this kid before. Sometimes he was taller and didn't have freckles, but in almost every school he'd be the first to try to make friends. Because he didn't have any friends. And I was beginning to see why. Here he was, grinning eagerly, actually hoping, you could tell, I'd known some movie stars, when I'd spent most of my time in L.A. bumming quarters at the video arcade. Sometimes I'd spend the whole night there, 'cause my mom had gotten into the habit of double-locking the door when she was "entertaining her friends."

It wasn't that he was a bad kind of guy, but I knew making friends with him wouldn't help me here. In fact it would make things worse. So I said, "Sure. I knew lots of movie stars. They were always coming by to swim in my pool."

"You had a pool?"

"Doesn't everyone in L.A. have a pool?"

"Never thought of that. You have a motorcycle too?"

"No." I couldn't go on with this.

He said, "My dad has a motorcycle. And he taught me how to ride. Then, well, his bike isn't running right now." More floor staring. "But I'm getting a Kawasaki KX500. For Christmas, I bet."

The bus pulled up in front of the school. The door wheezed open. Barry picked up his book bag, which appeared to weigh a ton, and squeezed his way into the aisle. But I hung back. I wasn't about to get off the bus with him.

I waited and got off the bus alone and was making my way toward the school when I saw what must've been the whole sophomore class gathered around Trevor and a girl with a lion's mane of hair. They were wrapped around each other, gazing out at their subjects. Barry was just joining the group.

When I got close, he turned and said, "Hey, did you guys know Alex is from L.A.? And guess what? Movie stars used to come swim in his pool!"

"Really? Who?" asked the girl. I thought her name was Denise.

"Christian Slater," I said, sneering with what I hoped was Christian Slater style.

"And you believed him," said Trevor. "What a dunce."

I could see I'd scored a point with Trevor, but Barry's shoulders sagged. He turned and started for the door. "Hey, don't go," Wyatt shouted after him. "We want to hear more about the movie stars."

It made for a sour victory. I watched him walk into the school with that overweight book bag dragging him down, and next thing I knew I was following him. I couldn't believe it, but I was. I walked faster and faster until I caught up with him. Then I was falling into step with him. Even though I couldn't think of a single thing to say.

From then on, I couldn't get rid of the guy. I thought it was pretty strange. I'd made a fool of him, but now he followed me everywhere. To my locker, to the john. The only good thing was that at lunch he rescued me from the cafeteria, took me over to a park a little way from the school. There he shared everything he'd brought, and he'd brought a lot. Grandma had packed a good lunch, but this kid had those cupcakes that come in plastic bags. Chips and candy bars too. All the extras without the sandwich. By putting our lunches together, we both came out pretty good.

But it was a pain to be around him. He was just too nice. Didn't he know it didn't pay to be this nice? In English, *Romeo and Juliet* again, he kept turning around to smile at me all through the dreary reading of the rest of Act II.

"So what happened here?" the teacher asked. She floated across the front of the room. "Denise?"

"There's a friar, right?" Denise tossed back that mane of hair. "Isn't that some kind of priest?"

"Yes," said the teacher. "And Romeo and Juliet went to the friar. Why did they do that?"

"It doesn't make any sense to me," said someone in the back.

"They got married," volunteered the girl who sat across the aisle from me, and the floater smiled, so she must've been right. Which was pretty remarkable. 'Cause I knew she hadn't been listening. I'd watched her draw three horses, one doing tricks on a skateboard, and two that looked like they were shooting pool in cowboy boots and cowboy hats.

Now someone challenged her. "How do you know? Where does it say that?"

"'Till Holy Church incorporate two in one,'" she said, without missing a stroke on those horses.

"That means they got married?" More than one kid echoed that thought. "Why doesn't it just say they got married?"

"I think Romeo's a jerk," said Wyatt.

Suddenly the class was quiet. But the teacher stayed remarkably calm. She floated over toward Wyatt and said, "Why do you think that?"

"'Cause he is." Wyatt sounded like he'd just as soon let the matter drop.

But the teacher peered out through her round glasses and said, "Does anyone else feel this way?"

Silence. Then, "Yeah." It was Trevor. "You know, tell me if I'm wrong, 'cause I'm having a hard time following this." This loosened the class back up. There were cheers from around the room. "Right on!" and "No kidding!" Until Trevor said, "Didn't Romeo meet Juliet just last night?"

This was news to me, but the floater said, "That's right."

Trevor sat up in his chair. "So what's he getting married for?"

"Yeah, why buy a cow when milk's so cheap?" This was Wyatt again, revived.

"No, that's not what I mean." There'd been a ripple of laughter, but it died. Trevor made it die. "Shouldn't he get to know her first? I mean, if I met some girl at a party and married her the next day, my parents'd have a fit. They'd think I'd gone nuts or something."

Wyatt looked sideways at Trevor. You could tell he couldn't believe his hero was talking this way in an English class. He said, "I'd think the girl had gone nuts." It was a desperate attempt to pull his friend back to reality, and it didn't work.

Even before this round of laughter had died, Trevor was saying, "I thought Romeo was in love with someone else. What was her name?"

"Rosaline," said the horse-drawing girl.

"But Rosaline didn't love him." This was a girl from the other side of the room who seemed suddenly concerned. "I mean, no matter how you feel about someone, if they don't care about you, there's really nothing there. But Juliet loves him too."

"And love can happen that fast." It was Barry who said this. "Romeo's not a jerk. When you love someone the way they do, you want to say so. That's why they get married. Maybe not everybody would. And times have changed, I guess. But they want everyone to know how much they love each other." He was talking fast, and loud, like he was daring anyone to tell him he was wrong.

"Except they don't tell anyone they got married." This was the girl with the horses again, and she said it much too softly for anyone but me to hear.

"What you been doing?" I asked her. "Reading ahead?"

Trevor said, "When it happens that fast, I don't think it's love."

"Really? What is it, Trevor? I bet you know all about that sort of thing." This was Denise, and where Wyatt had been unable to squelch Trevor's interest in Shakespeare, she was successful. The room convulsed with laughter, and Trevor didn't say anything more.

The floater made a few attempts to get him going again. Or someone going, anyone. But soon she must've realized the moment had passed. She told a couple of students to go back to reading, and we listened to the drone of their voices until the bell rang.

Chairs screeched against the floor. Notebooks slapped shut. We got out of that room so fast you'd think the desks had been set on fire.

"Hey, Barry, since when are you an expert on love?"

Wyatt was leaning against the drinking fountain. Barry was halfway down the hall at his locker. Wyatt wasn't really talking to him. He was making an announcement to the hall.

But Barry came toward him, defiant, and yelled back, "Maybe I know more than you think."

I'd kind of wanted a drink, but I couldn't believe this scene. Why did Barry say stupid things like that? Was he trying to make people not like him? I started drifting toward the other end of the hall.

"Tell me about all your true loves," Wyatt taunted him.

"You think you can just push everyone around," Barry shouted back.

Wyatt laughed. "I can sure push you around, but it's hardly any fun."

Then, even from the other end of the hall, I could see the gears shift in Wyatt's head. He glanced at me before turning back to Barry. "Hey, now I remember," he said. "You *are* pretty hot with the girls. And you've got a crush on that new girl. Alice? Isn't that her name?"

"You're a creep," said Barry.

"Whooa, a little touchy there."

"Not everyone is going to let you push them around. Alex is from L.A. He's not going to let a small-town punk like you push him around. And yeah, he's my friend."

By that point Barry had come close enough to

Wyatt I might not have heard him if I hadn't been listening, but everyone in the hall could hear what Wyatt
said next. "Hey, Alice. Is this true? Are you Barry's new
girlfriend?"

Suddenly the hall was quiet, and everyone was
turned toward me. I looked around at all those faces I
was only beginning to know, and I saw Barry, standing
proud, like now he had a champion. A gunfighter from
out of town. I had to admit I kind of liked that image of
myself. But one swing at Wyatt, and Hodson would be
on the phone. Next Driscoll would haul me off to
MacBride. So much for the rider from out of town.

I didn't know or care much about Romeo, but
Barry was definitely a jerk for putting me in this spot.

So I couldn't believe it when I heard myself say,
"Back off. Barry's a little weird, but he's OK. And yeah,
he's my friend."

Wyatt just looked at me for a moment. Down the
length of the hall our eyes locked. You could see he was
surprised and didn't have a quick comeback. Then the
corner of his mouth twitched upward.

And I knew what I'd already known, even before I'd said it. That nothing was going to happen now,
but I'd made another mistake.

Finally I was on the bus again. Watching Barry lope out to the football field. To be tackled by Wyatt probably. I could just imagine the bruises that kid must have. Why had a kid like that gone out for football? Anyway, I was glad to be rid of him. Glad to be away from Wyatt too.

Headed home. The word came to me by accident, and, maybe for the first time in my life, it felt good.

"You were great." The girl who drew horses was dropping into the seat beside me. "Alex. That's your name, isn't it? Not Alice."

I just looked at her. Guess I was feeling a little gun-shy after the disaster of making friends with Barry. And she wasn't the kind of girl that got my attention. Not that she was *bad* looking, but she wasn't wearing any of the makeup or jewelry I was used to seeing girls wear, and instead had on one of those flannel shirts like the guys here wore.

You could tell it made her uncomfortable, though, me not saying anything. She said, "Sandy had a horse thing to go to," almost like an apology. Sandy must've been the girl she usually sat with. "That's all she lives for, her horses. She's grooming them or showing them. But I just like to ride them."

By then I'd decided I was being an idiot. A girl like her wasn't going to cause me problems the way Barry had. I said, "Seems you like to draw them too."

"You noticed!"

You could tell she was surprised, and pleased, I'd been watching her draw. But you couldn't help it. It was the most interesting thing happening in that class. I said, "They're kind of funny-looking horses, though."

"Yeah, I know." She did this kind of embarrassed grin. "Guess they're more like cartoon animals. I mean, I like to draw them doing things. With clothes on and all. But my folks say, 'Don't think you can make a living drawing goofy animals.' They want me to do something 'practical,' like be a teacher or something. I'd sure like to prove them wrong." She paused, but just for a minute. "That's why I liked you saying what you did."

I'd been following the stuff about her parents, but this . . .

"About Barry," she explained. "'Cause he really is kind of weird."

That made me laugh. What was funny was the way she didn't say it funny, but very serious.

"He is," she insisted, still very serious. I tried not to laugh again. "But he has a right to be weird. We don't

all have to be like Trevor. And Wyatt can be a pain. I
have a right to draw funny-looking animals if that's
what I want to do, and you have a right to have long
hair and wear that silly earring if that's what you want."

That stopped me. Was she putting me down?

But she quickly said, "I'm sorry. I mean, your
earring isn't silly. I shouldn't say that. Probably lots of
guys wear them in the city."

I said, "People wear all kinds of different things
in the city," thinking, is there some kind of rule here you
have to wear flannel shirts?

She kind of shrugged. "Yeah, well, it's hard to be
different in a small town like Rimrock. I mean, I like it
here. I know everyone here. When I think about leaving, maybe going to a school where I can study drawing, it scares me to think about being surrounded by all
those people I don't know. But I guess that's the way
Rimrock is for you. And Rimrock, well—I mean it isn't
a secret—sometimes we're not very nice about letting
new people in."

I looked at her again. She really was different
from most of the girls I'd known. But I was beginning
to like the difference. I said, "You're sure right about
that."

She said, "By the way, my name is Mickey, like
the mouse." Then, while the bus was bouncing up and
down those gravel roads, dropping off the same stream
of kids it had picked up in the morning, we had this . . .

conversation. I mean, it was easy talking to her. Maybe because she wasn't the kind of girl that got my attention, and made me all nervous.

And she was sure good at talking to me. She told me how Mrs. Clausen, the floater who taught us English, said there was a whole field called illustration that maybe she could work in someday. I didn't have anything like that to say about myself, but I told her how this guy I used to know had sold a cartoon to a magazine.

She also told me about all the kids on the bus — she really did know every one of them — and who their parents were, and who their parents' parents were too. What was weird was the way everybody seemed to be related to just about everybody else, like there were just a few big families living out here like clans. "They're really Eckerts," she'd say. At least a third of the kids on the bus were some kind of cousin of hers, third or fourth, or twice removed.

Then she started talking about Rimrock, and how a lot more people used to live out here. Because of the Homestead Act. They thought it was a pretty good deal when the government gave them these chunks of land, but then they couldn't make it. Because the land was so dry.

"See that building there?" she said. We were passing a small white building with a tower for a bell. Some of the windows were broken, and the roof was sagging in. "More than sixty kids used to go to that school. Now I don't think there's a hundred and fifty at the Rimrock School. That's kindergarten through high school. And there used to be two-room schools like that all over the place."

I looked out at the empty field we were passing. "Where did all those kids live?"

"Maybe right there," and she pointed at nothing at all. "There used to be a lot more houses here, and even towns with city streets, and ice cream parlors and grocery stores. When the towns were abandoned, people burned them down, plowed them under, planted wheat."

"No skyscrapers, I guess."

"Or freeways," and she laughed. "They were biodegradable towns. But up in the woods, well, I guess up there they never planted wheat. So some of the old homesteads are still standing."

"Really?" I'd been enjoying imagining the way this place must've looked, with smaller farms and lots of little towns, but this really got my attention.

"Yeah, there's a couple of old homesteads right above where you live."

"Where I . . . ?"

"Don't you live with the Russels? Aren't they your grandparents?"

I hadn't thought about the fact that since she knew so much about everyone here, she probably knew about me. Did she know I was "really a Shafer"? How much did she know about me?

But she didn't give me time to think about that. She said, "Effie and Leland are great. I used to go over there all the time, and Effie would give me cookies. She makes the best cookies. Then I'd go on up into the woods and explore the homesteads up there. Would you like to see those places? One of them's pretty close."

"Sure." An old homestead right above my grand-parents' house! It would be like having a piece of the dream where I could walk to it.

"Great!" said Mickey. Then, "Here's where I live. Guess I've got to get off. But I'll be right over. OK?"

I was stunned. I said, "OK."

I was sitting at the kitchen table, eating peanut butter cookies this time — Mickey was right about Grandma's cookies being the best — and I couldn't believe my luck. Grandma had said I didn't have to work, not if Mickey wanted to take me to an old homestead. My only worry was that Mickey wouldn't show up.

Then I saw her ride into the yard — on a horse! She swung down, slipped off the saddle and bridle, slung them over the fence, and put the horse in the corral with Matilda, Grandma's milk cow. Soon after that I was walking up the gravel road I'd driven the day before, feeling this girl was some kind of guide leading me into one of my dreams.

"How far are we going?" I asked.

"Into the woods and then up a little, and then over, and . . . you'll see."

The cows out at the end of the field were just small brown humps. But we reached the wooden gate a lot quicker than I'd thought. Mickey really walked. If

I'd ever walked that far before, I'd sure never done it that fast. I figured we would've passed about twenty-five blocks' worth of houses and apartments and grocery stores, and me and my friends would've had to stop a bunch of times.

Then Mickey climbed up the slats of the gate and dropped down on the other side.

There it was completely different. There was still a road, but it didn't have gravel on it, and didn't look like it had been driven for a long time. It was covered with a layer of pine needles and twisted back and forth between the trees. It seemed less a road than a trail made for wagons and horses. I could imagine the fields built up into city streets, but this I couldn't. It was almost like the place was magically preserved. Cut right out of one of my books.

Mickey began to walk slower. There was something about this place that made you want to walk slower. And quieter too. Out in the fields we'd been talking the way we had on the bus, and she'd been telling me some of the same stuff Grandpa had about the drought. But now she didn't say much. So I didn't say much, and just listened to the quiet as we went on up that road. Then Mickey turned off onto a path, and we followed the path until she leaped across a ditch, and we came out into a clearing.

She grinned, "Pretty neat place, don't you think?"

But all I could see was a building smaller than

Grandma's chicken coop, with a hole in the roof so it wouldn't even keep a guy dry. It was maybe twelve foot square, made of thin boards, not logs, and the floor was gone. You could see where the floor had been. The joists were still there, but the planks of the floor had been pulled up.

I stood in the doorway and couldn't believe I'd walked all that way to see this.

There were a couple of beer cans lying in the dirt and what looked like the remains of a campfire, a few of the planks pulled up from the floor that were piled and charred in the middle of this shack, or shed, or whatever it was. It couldn't ever have been a house.

Mickey said, "It's a shame, I know. Some people don't have any respect. And this place is so close to the road. Anyone can find it. Still, I really like it. Don't you?"

I looked around and shivered. "People lived here?"

"Sure, what's it look like? Come on, I'll show you the cistern," and she took me to a place where a couple of boards lay on the ground. She lifted one, and below it there was an empty hole about twenty feet deep. It was lined with rock, and it looked like a well, but there wasn't any water in it. "They had to carry their water in, in wagons. There are just a few springs around here. Then they'd pour it in here."

"And drink it?"

"Of course. I mean, they had to. I bet the creek runs only a couple of months a year."

"What creek?"

"The one we jumped across. Over there."

I turned to look at the ditch. And something went click in my head. 'Cause that dry ditch wasn't a creek to me, and this was nothing like any of the cabins in my dreams.

My face must've shown her what I thought of the place.

She said, "You know, the people who came here, I bet they were disappointed too. I mean, it isn't exactly Iowa. A hundred sixty acres of this"—and her hand swept out to include the little clearing and the trees around it— "well, no one could make a living on it. My dad says it was kind of a mistake on the part of the government. People came here with big dreams, then, like I said, most of them gave up. Went on to the Willamette Valley where things were easier."

Coming here with big dreams. These people had been a lot like me.

"There's another homestead up farther," she said, "that I like even better than this. I bet you would too. It's a lot more like a house. But this is a kind of special place too. Over there, by the front door, in the spring, there are daffodils."

The front door? There was only one door.

"Daffodils," she said, pointing, as if that made it

clear. "The woman who lived here planted daffodils. Then, when she looked out her window"—there really wasn't any window, just a square hole in one wall— "and she saw those daffodils coming up, she knew she'd done something."

I looked at her, still not understanding.

"In the spring I'll have to show you," she said. "She really did do something. The daffodils are still here."

Coming here with big dreams. For the next few days I couldn't get that out of my head.

And I'd think of my mom, the way she was each time we moved.

During the packing and driving—she always packed everything in one day and drove all night— she'd be pretty hysterical. Crying and yelling at me. Blaming everyone for every stoplight that slowed us down. But as soon as we got a new place to live, she'd unpack her stereo first, put on a tape, and start singing along. She'd grab me and try to get me to dance with her. When I was younger I would. Even though all those places were dumps, with so much dirt ground into the floor and walls you couldn't tell what color they were, she'd say this one was better than any of the rest and put up these few scraggly treasures of hers. One I now realized was a picture of the mountain you could see from the attic room. Then she'd say, "Finally I'm away from that . . ." boss, boyfriend, landlord—just fill in the blank. "Alex, I promise, things are going to be so much better here."

Now I was making my own promises. Lying to myself.

While stabbing stuffed animals, nearly setting that counselor's office on fire. And guaranteeing I'd have to have it out with Wyatt. That must've been my reason for standing up for Barry.

Lately it seemed I never knew why I did anything.

How could I have ever thought things would be different here? As if I could be that eight-year-old again. I never got in trouble when I was eight.

Maybe I should just call Driscoll and tell him, "You're right. I'm no good. I'm not going to make it here."

But I couldn't do that.

So I kept on with the "regular school attendance," and made sure I was never near Wyatt when there wasn't a teacher around.

Jake wasn't fully pleased. Counselors never are. He'd call me in and complain about my "lack of participation" in my classes. "You know, it's not our intention just to detain you here. We'd like to educate you too. And I bet Mr. Driscoll expects a little better performance from you."

"No," I said. "Attendance, that's it."

It was nice to have Mickey talk to me once in a

while at school, and Barry was still being friendly, of course. But all I was hoping for there was survival. And when I wasn't at school, things were amazingly good.

Instead of getting up to find some guy stalking around the kitchen in his underwear, just as unhappy to see me as I was to see him, there'd be Grandma in her sweats—unless she had to go to town, she always wore sweats. And I could hardly see her in them without remembering the way they used to feel when we'd sit together on the couch and she'd read to me, that summer, back before I could read to myself. Anyway, as soon as she saw me, she'd say something, something nice—she never yelled at me—and she'd give me great things to eat.

Then after school I'd do something with Grandpa, feed the cows or fix a fence. Stuff like the guys in my books always did. Grandpa still called me a city kid, but that didn't bother me anymore. I could actually feel myself getting stronger. I was also getting pretty good at driving the truck.

Sometimes I'd think about my dad, and wonder why he hadn't shown up. But I'd lived without him a long time. And after a couple of weeks of that, I'd almost forgotten the way I'd felt when Mickey had shown me that cabin that was hardly a cabin at all, just some kind of tombstone left from someone's dead dream.

Then my birthday came.

And my birthday started out really good. Great,

in fact. Grandma fixed these big apple pancakes that she baked in the cast-iron frying pan, and they grew up the sides of the pan until they were brown and crisp and made the whole house smell of apples and cinnamon.

There were also two presents on the table that morning. One was the state driver's manual. Grandma said, "Now that you're fifteen, you can get your learner's permit." Grandpa said, "It's about time I had me a chauffeur." In the other package there was a jacket, a really warm jacket. Something I'd been wishing for in the mornings. Now sometimes even at noon it was cold. The jacket was a little more red and green than things I usually wore, but I thought it was maybe the first jacket I'd had with long enough sleeves.

So it started out like that, the way you think birthdays are supposed to be. And since it was a Friday, even though I had to go to school, it wasn't too hard to make it through the day. Then when I got back home, I found Grandma bent over a recipe book. She had peppers of five different colors, tortillas, tomatoes, three kinds of cheese, and several new bottles of spices all over the kitchen table. Beans and some kind of meat were simmering on the stove. She said, "Didn't you say you liked enchiladas?"

"Yeah!" I did like enchiladas a lot. I liked all kinds of Mexican food, and it wasn't the kind of thing Grandma usually fixed.

"I made a coconut cream pie for you too."

Then I knew, if this was really *my* birthday, not some other kid's, this couldn't be what was happening.

Grandpa had said I didn't have to work, but I half wished I did. 'Cause all I could do was lie across my bed in my room with years of other birthdays rolling through my head.

I found myself remembering the time my mom had said we'd go to the zoo. I'd never been to a zoo. So she told me all about it, acting it out, making me laugh the way she could. "We're going to see the bears," and she growled like a bear. "We're going to see the monkeys," and she jumped up and down going "Ooog ooog." For weeks she went on like that.

On my birthday when we got in the car, she was still doing her animal imitations. Until we pulled up in front of a house. "I'll just be a minute," she said.

So I waited. I waited so long I fell asleep.

Finally she came out. But she wasn't alone. "Alex, get in the backseat. Hal's going to ride up front." She spent the rest of the day and late into the night driving that guy all over town, stopping at one house after another, and each time leaving me in the car. At one point I dared to say, "What about the zoo?" "This is important," she said. "We'll have to do that some other time. And don't you start your whining, or I'll leave you right here on the street. You know I can't drive when you're whining." And Hal said, "Why do you want to go there? It's a prison for animals. A place to stay away from, kid."

Of course, I was too young then to understand what she must've been doing at all those houses. I didn't understand any of her ups and downs then. Or the way she could forget things, just completely forget things.

Like the time she said, "When you get home from school, you and I are going to have a party. I've already got all the streamers and stuff, and I'm going to rent one of those game machines. Will you teach me how to play?"

All that day I kept wondering which games she was going to rent. I'd given her a whole list of them, knowing she couldn't get them all. But when school was finally over, and I got to go home, she wasn't there. I let myself in, thinking she must be getting that game machine. 'Cause the streamers were up. A "Happy Birthday" balloon bounced from the arm of a chair.

But again I just waited and waited. At least I wasn't trapped in a car. I'd given up and gone to bed before I heard her come home. I heard her giggling with the man she was with while they were still out in the hall. Then, after a lot of fumbling with the key, they got the door open, and the giggling stopped. "Oh," she gasped. "I forgot." She must've seen the balloon.

Then there was the time one of her boyfriends decided he'd do my birthday. Take me to a basketball game. But after a while he decided I wasn't having as good a time as I should. Since he'd spent all that money on those tickets. I thought I was enjoying the game, but

I was always quiet around my mom's boyfriends. And that one, by the time we got home, did a full-scale demonstration of why I was right not to trust them. My mom tried to defend me. She had this thing that only she had the right to hit me. Which was kind of strange, but easier to understand than the way she let them hit her.

Yeah, there were lots of things about her I still didn't understand.

Of course, my birthdays weren't always like that. Sometimes she'd get into celebrating with me. But when my mom is "celebrating," she can go from pleasant to nasty in five seconds flat. I spent my seventh birthday in the emergency room 'cause she'd come at me so crazy I had to get three stitches in my head.

So as I got older I learned not to trust her birthday promises. She'd point out something in a store window, or maybe in an ad on TV, and say, "How'd you like that for your birthday?" and I'd know not to let myself dream about it. She'd ask me, "What do you want to do for your birthday?" and I'd tell myself I was just playing into her game, letting her have an edge on me, if I said anything. So I'd try to say, "Just forget it." But I was never really able to forget it, and not give her anything to promise me, and hold over me. As my birthday got closer and closer, I'd feel the two parts of me pulling at each other. The hopeful part and the part that knew she was going to trick me again.

Until I was pulled so thin and tight, that morning I'd confront her. "Hey, it's my birthday. Bet you can't wait to screw it up." She'd go into her you-don't-appreciate-anything-I-do-for-you routine. And I'd stalk off to school, sure to be in the office before noon. The school would call to tell her I was suspended for the next three days, and that would give her a great excuse to "cancel" whatever she claimed to have planned for me.

I hadn't even bothered going to school on my last birthday. I'd gone downtown, convinced a drunk to buy me some tequila, and hung out in the park with a bunch of guys until one of them said something—no telling what—and I decided to show him not to mess with me. Then someone called the cops. Assault, criminal trespass, minor in possession, and resisting arrest.

I had to think of something else.

That was when I began to wonder if my dad might come. The way everyone here seemed to know all about everyone else, by now he had to know I was here. He had to know when my birthday was.

Then I heard a car pull in. And Grandma go out onto the porch. I listened, half eager to run down and see him. Also half scared.

Until I heard Grandma say, "Linda, I'm so glad you could come."

I felt my whole body go stiff.

"How was the drive?" Grandma's voice was

louder than normal. Kind of nervous and formal. I realized they'd hardly seen each other since I was born.

"Long," said my mom. "And this car. The guy I
bought it from told me it got thirty-five miles to the gal-
lon. So, of course, it got maybe half that."

I was always amazed at the way she thought
everyone else was a liar.

"Well, I'm just glad you decided to come."
Grandma's words were so honest you could feel it in
your bones.

It made me kind of sad, hearing that, and thinking of how little she'd seen us. Once in a while my mom
would call her and let me talk on the phone, and
Grandma would always say, "When am I going to see
you?" But even though visits were planned—my mom
was a master at making big plans—she was also a master at excuses.

I could remember only one time Grandma had
actually come.

And Grandpa hadn't. My mom had said, "You
can come if you don't bring Dad."

Grandma had planned to stay two weeks. But
the first thing she did was scrub the place clean. "Linda,
I know I raised you better than this." She gave away the
clothes that didn't fit me anymore and bought me new
ones. She took me to a dentist, shocked to find I'd never
been to one. "If you need money, we'll gladly help out.
We want Alex to see a dentist every six months, and

have clothes that fit. Linda, there's nothing wrong with accepting a little help." My mom made sure she was back on the bus in less than a week, and wasn't about to let her visit us again.

So why had my mom come here today? It couldn't have been an easy thing for her to do.

You'd think she'd have a hard time facing me too.

"Alex," Grandma called up the stairs. "Your mother is here." As if I didn't know.

I forced myself to get up off the bed, but before I started down the stairs, I grabbed my new jacket. 'Cause already I could feel my brain starting to shift, into that place where I never knew what it was going to do next.

As soon as my mom saw me, she did this terrific smile of hers. Smiling like that, she came toward me like she was going to hug me. One look at me must've told her that wasn't going to happen. She stopped and said, "You're looking good. You've gotten a tan out here."

Did she think that made everything right?

I said, "I'm doing OK."

Grandpa was also in the living room. Sitting in his favorite chair. But holding the newspaper so tight you could see every vein in his arm.

My mom turned to him. "Daddy, you don't look happy to see me."

"Surprised is all," he said.

Grandma said, "Didn't I tell you she might come? If she could get away from her new job. Didn't you say you had a new job? Down in Reno? How do you like it there?"

Grandpa said, "Gettin' a job is a whole lot different from keepin' one."

My mom's back straightened. "I thought it would be nice to visit. You know, I haven't seen you and Mom for a while," and, after only a moment's hesitation, she did her smile again.

She used to be really good-looking. I'd seen pictures of her when she was good-looking, with this thick, curly, blond hair. Now her hair was neither thick nor curly, and barely blond. 'Cause she couldn't do a thing for herself anymore was what she said. Her face was thin, her neck was thin too. Her eyes looked out of purple hollows. But when she smiled, she still looked good. Men still thought she looked good.

But Grandpa must've seen her smile as much as I had, and become immune. He said, "Don't think we haven't noticed just how long it's been."

"Daddy, you haven't changed a bit."

Grandma said, "There's been a lot of water under the bridge." Then she made a show of taking my mom's coat. "Here, I'll put this up for you. And Alex, there's a plate of chips and things in the kitchen. Would you please get it for me?"

But I didn't move. I just held that jacket tighter and tighter.

My mom looked around the room and said, "I thought Bruce might be here."

"I asked him to come," Grandma called from the hall closet. "But he said . . . " She came back into the living room, glancing at me as she did. "Well, I guess it wasn't a good time for him."

Grandpa said, "You never could learn that you gotta live with the things you done. You ran him off. Now leave him alone."

Grandma said, "Please. Let's talk about something else."

Grandpa said, "At least that explains why you came. Guess I should've known. It wouldn't be us you wanted to see. Or your son."

I couldn't wait any longer. Guess Grandma wanted out of there too. The two of us got tangled up in the doorway to the kitchen. Then she went over to the chips and pretended to be doing something with them. But I could see tears in her eyes.

I went on past her and out the back door.

Soon I reached the wooden gate, climbed it, and dropped down into the woods. It was a lot darker under the trees, but by then my eyes had gotten used to the dark. I went on up the old dirt road, and I found the place where the path turned off. I'd been afraid I might not be able to, but I did, and after a while I could see moonlight shining into the clearing. I made my way toward it, almost fell into the ditch Mickey had called a creek, but found the cabin finally, just a small square shape in the night.

Even though it wasn't the way I'd dreamed a cabin in the woods would be, it was somewhere to go when I needed somewhere to go. I sat where the floor should've been, zipped the jacket up all the way to the neck, flipped up the collar, and wondered how long it would be before my mom left. At least with the jacket I was warm.

But after a while, the wind came up. I heard it in the tops of the trees. It also blew through the thin board walls. I began to wish the jacket was larger, more the size of a sleeping bag.

In front of me was the charred pile of boards. For a long time I stared at it. Then, when it seemed I couldn't stand the cold any longer, I remembered a few days ago I'd managed to pick up a package of matches.

10

When I got back to the house, it was almost dawn. I went around to the front to see if my mom's car was still there, ready to go back to the woods if it was. It wasn't, so I went in and up to my room, buried myself under all of my blankets, and went right to sleep.

By the time I woke up, I could tell it was the middle of the day. And no one was in the house. I stumbled down to the kitchen and felt how I was the only one there. By this time Grandpa was usually out doing something, and Grandma must've been too. Out with the chickens maybe. I could hear them carrying on. Matilda was leaning against the gate of her corral making noises too, mournful sounds I'd never heard her make before. I wondered if there was something wrong with her. But Grandma would know what to do.

I rummaged through the refrigerator, and there was the coconut cream pie. No one had cut into it, so the party must not have gotten any better after I'd left. I scooped a huge piece of it onto a plate, amazed that

Grandma could actually make something like that. Soon I was even more amazed. It was nothing like the frozen ones.

Just as I was finishing the piece of pie, the pickup truck drove in. It didn't go all the way into the garage but stopped at the kitchen door. Through the kitchen window I saw both Grandma and Grandpa get out, with Grandma getting out the driver's side. Something I'd never seen before.

Then Grandma came up to Grandpa and took his arm when he started up the steps. I could see him try to shake her off, but she held on. When they came in the kitchen door, she was still holding onto him. Until she saw me. She said, "Alex! You're here!" then seemed really torn about which of us to hover around.

Grandpa took this opportunity to get away from her. He said, "I told you he'd be here. He was probably here in bed by the time you'd drug me to that hospital." Then to me, "You just needed a little walk, didn't you?"

"Hospital?" I said.

Grandma said, "Maybe, but he never answered the phone. And they said . . . Oh, Alex, don't do that. We're supposed to call Mr. Driscoll if you run away."

"Why did you go to the hospital?" I asked.

"You did the right thing," Grandpa said. He settled into the chair across from me. "Wish I could've left too, and missed out on all the runnin' around and screamin' and fussin', and drivin' like a maniac into town. If that's the way your grandmother drives, she's not touchin' the truck again."

"Then coming home you kept saying I was going too slow."

"'Cause I wanted to get here before Christmas."

"Well, at least you came back," Grandma said to me. "And maybe you were right to leave. I'm so sorry, Alex. I never thought it would be like that."

"Will you just stop that sorry stuff!" Grandpa shouted this. It made both me and Grandma stare at him. "I'm just tired of you sayin' you're sorry for every damn thing. No wonder Linda thinks it's all our fault. You think it was."

"I don't know about that," said Grandma. "I guess I'll never know. But I do know this, a man your age should be able to let bygones be bygones. When Linda said she'd come, I so hoped . . . Leland, she's our daughter. Our only child."

"Don't you think I know that?"

The two of them stopped for a moment then, just looking at each other kind of sad. So I got a chance to ask again, "Why did you go to the hospital?"

Grandpa turned back to me. "It was nothin'. Your grandmother here, she decided I was dyin'."

"He had an angina attack."

"Which is nothin'. They gave me some pills."

"Well, it isn't as simple as that," Grandma insisted.

"They let me leave," Grandpa said.

"You refused to stay!"

"Still, they let me leave."

"He's supposed to avoid stress," Grandma said to me. "And I guess I'm going to have to start cooking differently. Maybe I should just sell old Matilda, and the chickens too. Which reminds me." She looked out the window, and there was Matilda still rubbing against the gate. "I forgot all about her." She turned back to Grandpa. "You take care of yourself." Then she grabbed the milk bucket and left.

Grandpa leaned toward me. "Don't you pay too much attention to her. I'm gonna be just fine. I just wish you'd cut me a piece of that coconut cream pie."

While I was at it, I got another piece for myself. Then for a while there was no reason for either of us to talk. Until all of a sudden Grandma came running back into the house. And I mean really running, something you don't often see a woman her age do.

"There's smoke up there!" she said.

Grandpa stood up and went over to the window. She said, "You can see it better from the barn." Then she was rushing to the phone, and Grandpa was going on out to the barn and peering up toward the woods. Grandma hung up the phone and said, "The lookout already spotted it." At almost the same time about eight Forest Service trucks pulled in, one with a pumper and another with a trailer carrying a huge Caterpillar. They drove on past the hay shed, turned up the narrow gravel road, and roared on up toward the woods.

Grandpa came running back into the house.

"Take it easy," said Grandma.

"Take it easy! There's a fire up there! And it hasn't rained since March! The wind's blowin' too."

A fire? A forest fire? I couldn't help thinking about the campfire I'd built.

But I knew I'd put it out.

"Alex, you can wear those old boots in the hall closet."

"You're not going up there," said Grandma.

Grandpa said, "I took my pills."

I found I was also rushing around. I got the boots out of the closet. They weighed something close to a ton. Then I clumped along behind Grandpa out to the machine shed and helped him throw all kinds of tools into the pickup. Next we were following the dust left by the Forest Service trucks. You could smell the smoke and see it rising from some distance up the hill.

The gate into the woods was open, but one of the Forest Service men wouldn't let Grandpa drive in. "We don't want any more vehicles up there." I heard a snap and a crash, and a burst of flame leaped from where the smoke had been. The man was talking into a radio, and then he was talking to Grandpa, then into the radio. It was hard for me to keep what he said all straight. A helicopter with something like a huge diaper hanging under it scooped up water from the pond at the end of the field and rose with a deafening noise, scattering cows and dust. The diaper thing swayed from side to side, and the whap, whap, whap of the blades carried it over us and up the hill.

Grandpa said, "Come on." The man must've told him what to do. He parked the truck, and we grabbed some tools that looked something like hoes, then started up the road, leaping off the road whenever a truck roared by.

We reached a place where men and women were tearing at the ground with tools like the ones we'd brought. Here the fire was just an orange line snaking its way through the trees. The Forest Service crew was beating at it, and we joined them, ripping at the ground. Tearing away everything, even the fine layer of needles, until there was nothing left but bare, brown dirt.

The smoke was so thick it burned my eyes and made it hard to breathe. I saw some of the firefighters had tied handkerchiefs over their mouths. I didn't have a handkerchief. I coughed my way along, beating at the ground and feeling I wasn't doing anything at all. If we stopped the fire from going one way, it turned and went in another direction. The heat burned my face and hands. As hot as it was, I didn't dare take off my shirt. I just let the sweat soak it and wished there was a breeze. But the wind had died. Someone said, "Thank God the wind has died."

Meanwhile, off to the side I could hear the growling of the Cat and the snapping and crashing of the trees falling in its path. Also every now and then there was the whir of the helicopter, next the slosh of the water falling, and a hiss when it hit the flames. At one point someone said, "We've got a line around it." Later, someone else came through and said, "We got the crown fire out." But still, all that afternoon I beat at the ground. Once in a while someone passed a water jug to me, but otherwise I kept on beating and scraping at the orange fingers that crept between the trees.

And I watched Grandpa beside me working just as hard. This wasn't good for Grandpa, I thought.

But I didn't want to think too much.

The helicopter had quit coming, and it had been a long time since there'd been a flash of flame, or the crash of a tree falling. Mostly there was just blackness where the orange fingers had been. Blackness and occasional puffs of smoke, but we still beat at the ground where there was any smoke. Some of the firefighters now wore water bags on their backs and sprayed down the places that were still hot. We worked our way through the woods that way.

Until we came to the place where the old cabin had been.

The forest had felt so different, with all the people and all the trucks and the fire and the smoke, I'd been able to tell myself the cabin might be farther up the

road, or maybe not as far. The clearing was also completely changed. Trees lay in it like pick-up sticks, and
everything was black. But now I could see the dry ditch
and the hole of the cistern.

I had to quit pretending I didn't know where I
was.

A Forest Service woman was studying the
ground. Grandpa went over to her, and the two of them
squatted down. I didn't have to hear them to know what
was being said.

That this was where the fire had started. Last
night, when I was here.

Again I remembered how I'd pulled the fire
apart. Then I'd covered it with dirt. But not well
enough, I knew now. Not well enough at all.

Grandma had heated up the enchiladas. They sat in the center of the kitchen table as untouched as the pie had been. "Help yourself, Alex," she said.

I forced myself to put some on my plate. Grandma had gone to a lot of work to make these for me.

Grandpa ignored the enchiladas. "Where'd you go last night?"

"Down the road," I said.

"What road?"

"The road. You know, the one that goes to town."

"You didn't go up into the woods?"

"No. It was dark. I just walked along the road." I managed to get some food on my fork, but I couldn't put it in my mouth.

Grandma served herself and said, "You both worked really hard today. You both must be hungry." She pushed the dish toward Grandpa.

He still ignored it. "When your grandmother here decided we had to go to town, we didn't see you on the road."

"I sat down under a tree for a while." Then I was trying to remember if there were any trees on the road to town. But Grandpa didn't challenge me on that. So I filled it in some, the way my mom would. "I think I fell asleep. I didn't see you either."

Grandpa said, "Our place could've burned. Mickey's parents' place could've burned. And the Dennison place. There's no way of knowin' how far it might've gone. When it's dry like this, a fire can burn till it rains."

I looked down at my plate. I knew what I'd done. But I couldn't admit it.

No matter how much I hated liars.

Grandma was also looking down at her plate, and I thought the lines that carved her face were deeper than ever before. Then she took a bite of the enchiladas, even though you could tell it was almost as hard for her as it was for me, and she said, "I'm sure these were better yesterday. Keeping them overnight like that has dried them out."

Guess it was her way of reminding Grandpa what had happened the night before. 'Cause he finally looked at the enchiladas and said, "Maybe you're right. It was a rough night. And we did get the fire out before much harm was done. Let's just hope nothin' like this happens again."

Mickey came over on Sunday. She wanted to see what the fire had done.

"I've already seen it," I said.

"Right. You were up there fighting it. But I wish you'd come with me. Is the cabin really gone? I want to see it, but I don't want to go up there alone."

I said there was nothing to see. I wanted her to just go home. But she insisted, and soon I was going with her up into the woods.

"Nice jacket," she said. "Did you get it for your birthday?"

I grunted.

"Did you have a good birthday?"

I didn't even bother to grunt.

"You don't want to talk about your birthday?"

"Can't you just leave me alone?" Then I felt bad. It wasn't her fault. "I'm sorry. I guess . . ."

"It's OK," she said. "I'm upset by the fire too."

The gate was still open. Just inside was a Forest Service truck. The man in the cab nodded at us, and Mickey waved at him. Then we were walking up the dirt road. Which was completely changed. Mickey commented on this, on the way all the trucks had turned it into powder dust.

When we left the road, the charred stuff on the ground crunched under our feet. Mickey commented on this too. And how the trunks of the trees were black, but their needles were still green. Then we were seeing trees where only some of the needles were green. Many were red. Mickey said, "Most of these will survive."

"Are you sure?"

"Well, not all of them."

The forest got blacker and blacker. We came to the tangle of fallen trees that used to be the clearing. Then she stopped in front of the emptiness where the cabin had been.

"Someone must've been camping here."

"Yeah, I guess."

"Did your grandparents see someone come up here? There's only the one road." When I didn't answer, she said, "People are so stupid. I can't believe anyone would build a fire when it's been so dry."

Then she surprised me by saying, "I'm sorry."

"*You're* sorry?"

"I mean, I know you were disappointed by the cabin and all, but you would've grown to like it. It would've been a place for you to come."

"Yeah," I managed to say.

"You know," she said, "it's still early. We could go on up to that other homestead I told you about. It's a little too far for after school. But it's a lot nicer. I mean, different. I know you'd like it."

"I don't want to see it."

"What?"

I'd surprised myself too, but I insisted, "I don't want to see it."

"But you'd like it. I know this is awful, but it happens up here all the time. I mean, this time it was a stupid camper, but it could've been a lightning strike. It'll make you feel better to see how much of the forest is still green."

"Don't you get it? I don't want to see another homestead."

I started back toward the road, walking as quickly as I could through the fallen trees. I hoped Mickey wouldn't be able to keep up with me. I just had to get away from her. What was I doing with her anyway? When she wasn't the kind of girl I usually liked. And she wasn't coming on to me either.

Instead she was *showing* me things.

Things I destroyed as soon as I touched them.

"Alex, did I say something wrong?"

I could hear her crashing through the brush behind me. Close behind, she was too quick. She caught up with me, grabbed me by the arm, and turned me around.

"Alex." Then, softly, "It was you who did this. I should've known."

I turned away. But she wouldn't let go. In fact she put her arms around me, and I just stood there, feeling how stupid I must look with my arms at my sides, held by her arms.

Always stupid. Stupid all my life.

"Alex, it's OK."

How could anyone be so stupid? How could anyone build a fire when it was so dry?

"You're from the city. You didn't know." I could feel her head pressed into my back. "Really, everything will grow back. Except the cabin, of course."

This was the way all my dreams ended up. Just a black, ugly mess.

I found I couldn't hold the tears at all, no matter how tight I squeezed my eyes shut. I turned and buried my face in her hair. And I'd never held a girl like that. Before it had always been something I was trying to do. This was something else.

After a while I managed to let go, embarrassed. She'd seen too much.

But all she said was, "Come on. I'll show you that other place."

I couldn't argue anymore. All I could do was follow her back to the road, and then up the road, and soon we were past the part where the trucks had torn it up. We were past the blackness too. The ground was covered with needles again, above us the trees were green, and it did feel good to find so much of the woods was still like that.

We followed the road until it narrowed into a path, and forked, then forked again. Soon the trail got so narrow you could tell not many people came here. The land leveled off, and we were on a high ridge. Then we came to a creek, a real creek, and we followed the

water down. Until the forest opened out into a wide
meadow. Which was a complete surprise.

I could feel how we were still high in the woods,
but this was a meadow that asked to be lived in. And the
house that stood just up from the creek wasn't just a
one-room cabin with a tiny square for a window. It had
a second story, a porch, and windows of glass, most of
them still unbroken.

In the living room there was a stone fireplace
with a wide hearth. "Room for their boots to dry,"
Mickey said. She took me up a stairway to two tiny
rooms. "Where the kids must've slept." She led me all
over the house. The kitchen was small and dark, but off
it there was a large pantry where the woman must've
kept her rows of jars, just the way Grandma did. There
was also a bedroom on the main floor, and it actually
had wallpaper on the walls. It also had a large window,
but it was nothing like the windows in the living room.
The living room ran the whole width of the house, and
the wall across from the fireplace was a long row of windows that looked out on the creek, and also a barn, a
chicken coop, and a couple of sheds.

"How did they get in and out of here?" I asked.

"I told you there used to be more people here. So
there used to be more roads."

"It would've been great to live here," I said. "I
can't believe they left." Then, "I'll take really good care
of it."

Mickey smiled. "I know you will."

I looked at her smile, thinking how different it was from my mom's. And how pretty it was. It was like I'd never really seen her before. Like I'd never really seen any girl before.

Then I saw something else in her face. Maybe it was just the way the daylight filtered in through the windows that were covered with dust. Maybe it wasn't really there, this thing I thought I saw now. This thing I felt inside me. How was I to know if I was just fooling myself with more dreams?

But she didn't seem at all surprised when I kissed her.

I t turned out to be one of those kisses that
puts an end to some old witch's curse.

Here I'd done the worst thing I'd ever done—there
was no doubt in my mind about that—something that
could've killed people or burned down their homes. And instead of finding myself strip-searched and locked up, exactly the opposite happened. My life became better than it
had ever been.

To the kids at school I was no longer some kind of
long-haired weirdo Trevor and Wyatt had marked as un-
touchable. I was a hero who had helped to fight the fire.

And Mickey's boyfriend.

Even though some of the kids may have thought
Mickey was a little strange for drawing those funny pictures, I'd discovered what mattered here was being from
one of those hopelessly interwoven families. And Mickey
was. Barry, well, it turned out his family had never been
one of the in-group.

But Mickey was OK. So her boyfriend had to be
OK too. And even though it was hard for me to believe I
really was her boyfriend, that part was great.

Being the hero firefighter was more difficult.

"I should tell them the truth." I managed to say that to Mickey once.

But she said, "Knowing who did it won't change anything. Like I told you, there are fires up there all the time."

"I guess. At least they got it out," I said. 'Cause I didn't *want* to tell anyone. I sure didn't want Driscoll to know.

"Right," said Mickey. "Besides, you are a good person. It's OK for people to like you."

She said a lot of things like that, that left me feeling she really didn't know me at all. And once she got to know me better, she was sure to leave.

Still, I couldn't help but enjoy the way things had changed.

Even Trevor talked to me, which meant Wyatt left me alone. At lunch instead of going off with Barry to the park and having to listen to his goofy view of the world, I found myself in the bed of one of those pickups, Mickey beside me, riding off with a whole bunch of kids to a hamburger stand so far away we only had time to drive there and back. I still had the lunches Grandma packed me. And no money. But sometimes I'd do what I'd done with Barry and trade with the other kids, for maybe a Coke or fries.

Sometimes I still thought about my dad. Wondered if he ever thought of me.

But mostly I was just happy.

I should've known better than that.

———

My math teacher gave me the note. It was the last period of the day, and a Friday too, so I'd been watching the clock. Things weren't so good I didn't still watch the clock.

I passed Barry on my way out of the room. He said, "What's up?"

"Hodson wants to see me. I haven't a clue."

Next thing I knew, I was waiting by the secretary's desk, listening to her talk on the phone. And remembering the way Hodson had welcomed me to Rimrock. "Give me a reason. Anything." Had he come up with one? But I couldn't think of what.

Unless he'd figured out the fire. Was that possible? Or maybe he just wanted to tell me old football stories about my dad.

Sometimes I thought my dad must feel the same way Hodson did, that having me was about the biggest mistake he'd ever made, and that was why he hadn't made his appearance. I felt myself getting tighter and tighter. Winding up like a spring. Why'd this guy call me in if he wasn't ready to talk to me?

Finally his office door opened. He motioned me to come in. As I went in, Trevor walked out. Trevor didn't look at me.

"Sit down," said Hodson.

I sat down.

"Well, I'm not too surprised," he said. "I told Effie and Leland they were making a mistake. You can't make a pie out of rotten apples, no matter how much sugar you add."

I felt the spring wind tighter.

"It would be best if you returned it."

Was this guy going to just talk in riddles?

"There's no point in denying it. You went back into the locker room early today. I guess you had an appointment with Mr. McCauley, but still you had plenty of time. And Trevor was careless. No doubt about that. He shouldn't have left his Walkman lying out on the bench. But this is a clean country school."

Right, and I'm not a clean country kid. Finally I could see where he was going with this.

"Of course, I can understand Trevor being careless. Theft is not a problem we've had. And we're not going to start having problems like that. So let's just put it this way. I'm very close to having you exactly where I want you. Out of this school."

By then my insides were so twisted up, I felt if I made a wrong move, told this guy what I thought of his apple pies, and his whole damn school, I'd fly apart.

And I wasn't about to tell him I hadn't taken the Walkman either. He'd expect me to say that no matter what I'd done.

I concentrated on holding myself together.

Usually you don't have anything to lose, but things had been going so good.

Somehow I walked out of that office still in one piece.

See, Ms. Lloyd, I'm getting better.

And there was Barry.

He said, "What happened? I was worried. I mean, you didn't come back to class. So I said I had to go to the john. What did Hodson do?"

I saw he really was worried. Which was big of him when you thought about how little time I'd been spending with him lately. Anyway, it was good to have someone there to talk to right then, so I could let that spring unwind a bit.

I said, "Someone took Trevor's Walkman. Hodson figures he might as well blame me."

"Hodson, he doesn't like me either. He doesn't like anyone different. But you wouldn't do anything like that. I mean, I know you. You're not like that."

I shoved open the door and went outside thinking Barry was great for comic relief at a time like this. 'Cause I'd never been above shoplifting when that had been what was happening with my friends. And I was always slipping money out of my mom's purse. Or out of her boyfriends' wallets, for that matter, if I lucked into finding one lying around.

I just hadn't taken this Walkman. 'Cause I didn't want to be a thief *here*.

But Barry's belief in me was kind of nice. Naive as it was.

It turned out he was so naive he believed in truth too. He said, "So you don't have anything to worry about, right? I mean, if you didn't do it, they won't be able to prove you did."

I knew things weren't that simple. But maybe the Walkman would turn up. Whoever had taken it would show it to someone. Word would get around. Barry was right that they didn't have any evidence on me. Except that I'd walked through the locker room. I should've expected Hodson to blame anything that went wrong on me. Someone else must've walked through that locker room too.

By the time Mickey showed up at the bus, I'd convinced myself everything was going to be OK. And I'd slowed down enough to make only an offhand comment. "Hodson's trying to pin a stolen Walkman on me." She said the same thing Barry had. "He doesn't like anyone different." Then we made our weekend plans.

Mickey had to go to Portland on Saturday, and

Grandpa wanted me to work. But Sunday we could go to the homestead again. The new one, that was what I called it, the one I hadn't burned. And since Barry was still there, sitting in the seat behind us on the bus, and leaning in between us—there must not have been a football practice that day— it seemed only right to invite him along.

I had mixed feelings about that. All you had to do was say a few words to the kid and you couldn't shake him off your leg. Spending a day alone with Mickey would've been nice. But when Sunday came, it turned out to be an almost-like-summer sunny day, making it hard to believe Thanksgiving was less than a week away, and Barry let out a whoop as soon as he saw the homestead. Took off down the path in front of us, leaped up onto the porch, rushed in through the door, then out again, shouting about how much better it was than everything we'd said. How anything anyone could say about the place would never be enough, and how pleased he was we'd taken him there. Well, I couldn't help feeling I'd done something right for once.

We found some cans in the kitchen with old-fashioned pictures on them, and some newspapers laid in the walls of the attic. "Pioneer insulation," Mickey said. We pulled them out and tried to read them in the dark of those tiny attic rooms. The paper was yellow and sometimes broke apart in our hands. We found the dates were 1915 to 1928, and Rimrock had been a whole lot different back then. A train used to come to the town. There was even a picture of the turntable where the train was turned around. But now even Mickey didn't know where the train tracks had been.

Then we went back outside and sat on the porch, our backs propped up against the house and the sun so bright in our eyes we had to squint. And we got out the food we'd brought. I had some of Grandma's cookies that crumbled in our hands. Mickey had apples she said she'd picked just that day. They were green, but she said, "Believe me, they're ripe. Taste them," and when I did, the juice dripped down my chin. Barry'd brought potato chips, the super-giant-size bag.

The chips made me thirsty. Mickey said, "Here, have another apple," but I figured I'd just get a drink from the creek. The way the guys in my books always did, the way I always did it in my dreams. She insisted I'd better not. "Beaver fever," she said.

"The people who lived here must've drunk from the creek. Weren't there beavers back then?"

She said, "Maybe they got sick back then too. They got sick from all kinds of things. They died from things that wouldn't make us miss more than a few days of school. That's just the way things were."

"OK," and I gave up on the vision I'd had of cupping the ice cold water in my hands. Instead I took another apple, and it did quench my thirst.

"I'm sure glad you came here," said Barry.

"Yeah," I said, closing my eyes. I could feel Mickey's arm against mine, and it seemed we were meant to be like this, leaning close together in the sunshine like this.

"When I get my dirt bike, we'll be able to ride all over these woods."

"Yeah," I said again.

Then Barry said, "Why'd you come live with your grandparents anyway?"

It was a question I'd been expecting. I didn't let it ruin the good feeling of the day. "Didn't get along with my mom."

I hoped he wouldn't push it any further. He didn't. But he said, "What about your dad?"

"My parents are divorced." That seemed simple enough.

Then Mickey said, "I'm glad you came to live with your grandparents too. If you'd gone to live with the Shafers, you'd be way the other side of Rimrock. I couldn't ride Dufur that far."

Barry must not have noticed my name was Shafer before. He said, "Are they relatives of yours?" Then, "Hey, I used to hang out at the Shafers. Last winter when the woods was closed, my dad worked for Bruce Shafer. After school I'd ride the bus over there."

I could still feel the sun on my face and Mickey against my side, but it wasn't the same anymore.

"I'd hang out with Jenny. It was fun. I mean, even though she's younger than me."

How much younger, I wondered. How long had my dad waited to start his new family?

"Bruce is really nice. And rich. All the Shafers are rich. That's why I liked to go over there. Jenny has all kinds of stuff. Video games, remote control stuff. And they have this big house. You should've gone to live with them. I mean, if they're relatives of yours. You'd've had a dirt bike and everything."

Mickey said, "Cut it out."

"Why?" said Barry. "What's wrong?"

"Nothing," said Mickey. "I'm sorry, Alex. I shouldn't have mentioned them."

I couldn't sit there any longer. I had to do something. I stood up.

Mickey said, "Really, I'm sorry. I know you don't want to talk about them."

I turned to face her. "How do you know? What do you know?" My voice came out thin and tight.

"I just know . . . " She looked confused. "Alex, I'm really sorry. I just know Bruce Shafer's your dad."

"He is?" Barry stared at me. "Then why didn't you go live with him?"

I saw Mickey knew the answer to that too. And she'd known all along! So that's why she'd sat down beside me on the bus. The poor kid, his dad just up and abandoned him. Won't take him in even now.

Maybe that was all this had ever been, her feeling sorry for me.

Barry said, "Man, I wish Bruce Shafer was *my* dad."

And good old Bruce, everybody loved him. Besides that, now it turned out he was rich. But even if, years ago, he had wanted to get me back, and probably that was just more of my crazy dreaming, he'd made it really clear he didn't want to see me now. Maybe both my parents used to think they wanted me, but neither of them did now.

How had I tricked myself into thinking Mickey did!

"I mean, my dad, he's OK," said Barry. "When he's working. And hasn't been drinking too much. But . . ."

Mickey interrupted him. "Don't you know when to quit!"

"At least he's not lying." I felt all this stuff like hot lava inside me, running up and down my arms, looking for a way out. "All this time you've been lying to me."

My hands clenched and unclenched. They wanted to smash something. I grabbed the railing of the porch. It wasn't too strong anymore. I wrenched it free and held a four-foot piece of wood in my hands, with nails poking out of it. I watched Mickey shrink against the house, and Barry jumped up and backed away. For a minute I just stood there, half enjoying their fear. See, Driscoll is right about you after all. Then I turned and threw that thing as hard as I could, as far as I could. It hit a tree with a satisfying crash. I looked at the way the uprights that had held it now hung off the edge of the porch and thought about yanking each one of them free too. Maybe I'd toss the whole porch into the woods, stick by stick.

But that energy was gone.

I could feel Mickey coming up behind me. Again. But nowhere near as sure of herself this time. She wasn't going to try to put her arms around me. She just said, "I've never lied to you. But your dad, well, I thought you should be the one to bring him up, and if you didn't, that was OK."

I stepped off the porch, right through the broken pieces of railing, and went down to the creek, where I slumped to my knees. And she followed me.

Which was weird when you thought about it. My mom had never followed me. She'd just call the cops.

I reached into the cold water. I didn't drink it, but I let it flow over my arms. And I felt Mickey drop down behind me, and edge closer. But still not so close that she touched me.

She said, "I just didn't want to hurt you. I mean, I don't understand Bruce. But I've heard he was awfully young."

Yeah. I knew that. I'd thought about that. How it would be to have a kid when you were only eighteen.

Maybe it *was* the biggest mistake of his life. I let the water run higher on my arms.

"And I *am* glad you came to live with Effie and Leland. Or you and me . . ."

Then I did feel her hand on my back.

"We wouldn't have gotten to know each other. Not like this."

Her hand was light, uncertain, but warm.

I turned toward that warmth. Uncertain too. But wanting to believe her.

"**W**hy do you have that big old barn and only one milk cow?" I asked. We were sitting down to dinner that night.

"We used to have more milk cows," said Grandma. "We used to sell milk. Back when we were younger. But that's a lot of work."

"Didn't you have horses too?"

Grandma passed me the biscuits. "Linda had a horse."

I took a biscuit, and passed them on to Grandpa. "Pass the butter," he said.

"Very funny," said Grandma.

"You think I'm gonna eat my biscuits with this?" He sneered at the cube of margarine that sat in the middle of the table where the bowl of butter used to sit.

"It's been two weeks now," Grandma said. "Do we have to go through this with every single meal?"

Grandpa turned to me. "We don't need a milk cow no more. Might as well burn that old barn."

"Well, I was thinking," glad to finally find a way

back to the idea I'd come up with walking back down the trail that afternoon, "that it might be nice to have a horse."

"What on earth for?" said Grandpa.

"Well, because. Then I could ride up into the woods. You've got that big barn, and all that hay. A horse wouldn't be much trouble, would it?"

"A horse is a pain in the butt."

I turned to Grandma for support, but she frowned. "You don't need a horse."

"Well, no. I just thought it would be nice. What does a horse cost?"

"Too much," said Grandpa. "And that's just the beginning."

"But I'm working," I said, and I was. Almost every day. And not getting paid a cent. Which I hadn't complained about before, but . . .

Grandpa poked at the chicken on the platter. "What's this?"

Grandma said, "You know what it is."

"How come it looks like this?"

"I skinned it, and then I baked it. I didn't fry it."

"You say you're tryin' to keep me alive, but seems to me you're just tryin' to take all the fun out of life. I just might sneak behind the barn and have a smoke right now."

I made one last attempt. It had seemed like such a great idea. If I had a horse, Mickey and I could go up to the homestead any day after school. And in my dream I always rode one. I said, "Is there anything I could do to pay for a horse? Maybe I could get a job in town."

"Well, the first thing you could do," Grandpa finally turned his full attention on me, "is you could give that radio thing back to that kid you took it from."

I could feel my mouth drop open.

Grandma said, "Leland, I thought we agreed to wait on that." Then to me, "You really shouldn't ask about getting a horse. Horses are a sore point with your grandfather."

"Why? This is horse country." I could hear my voice rising. "Mickey has a horse."

Grandpa said, "Mickey don't steal."

"And what makes you think I took that Walkman?"

"It has to do with your mother," Grandma explained. "Your mother was crazy about horses, you know."

"And you had to give her every damn thing she wanted. Didn't matter if she'd take care of it or not."

"I really don't think this is a good time to ask," Grandma said to me.

"She never took care of nothin'. Not even her own damn kid. So now we gotta take care of him. I keep tellin' you it wasn't your fault. And you can't make up for it now if it was." Grandpa turned to me again. "I'm not gonna buy nothin' for someone who sits right here in my house and steals."

"Leland, please, don't get like this."

"Don't get like what? Go ahead and say it. You think it was *my* fault Linda ran off like she did."

Grandma looked down at the table for a minute. And the next time she spoke, her words were real slow and quiet and tight. "We're not talking about Linda now. We're talking about Alex. And we don't know he took that Walkman thing."

"That's what you say. You say we should just wait and see. Wait and see what? Wait and see if he steals somethin' else? You think I'm gonna have a heart attack 'cause my grandson's a thief?"

I couldn't believe this. The day before we'd dug the cattails out of the pond. Grandpa and I had worked side by side sliding in the mud. Things had felt so good. But Hodson must've told them on Friday, not today. How had Grandpa kept all this in?

He said, "Well? Did you take it or not?"

"Would you believe me if I told you I didn't?"

"That's not an answer. And we know you've stolen stuff. Done drugs, beat up people. I bet you started the fire too. I figure that was an accident, but it shows that no, I can't believe a word you say. And right now I can't think why I let you come here."

"Leland, you don't mean that!"

I had filled my plate with chicken, biscuits, potatoes, corn. Now I knew I couldn't eat it.

But I just went up to my room. I didn't punch

Grandpa in the face. I didn't tear up a porch railing. Or throw my plate through the kitchen window.

I didn't even walk out the door. And that was what I wanted to do. Not just go up in the woods and sit there for a while, but really get out of this place.

Starting when I was maybe twelve I'd done that a lot. After all, I could take care of myself. I sure didn't need my mom anymore. What did she do for me? She didn't even stock the refrigerator so that you could count on finding anything in there to eat. So instead of begging her to quit, or hiding in a closet trying to hold the door shut, which was about all I'd been able to do when I was younger, I'd leave. Get away.

It always felt good to get away.

But I knew this time Grandpa would call Driscoll. And the juvenile court doesn't think kids can take care of themselves. If you run away, they act like they have no choice but to lock you up.

Hang on, you have too much to lose, I told myself again. He'll get over this in time, the way he got over the giraffe. And I made myself go up to my room.

There I just tried to use the dream to get away instead. And listened to the beating of my heart until I fell asleep.

By morning clouds had moved in. It was so gray and cold the sunshine of the day before seemed from some other century. "Maybe it'll finally rain," was what Grandma said. "Feels like snow to me," said Grandpa. At least it was the clouds they talked about at breakfast, not me. But as I waited for the bus, I felt those clouds pressing down, like things were closing in on me.

And they were. Even worse than I knew.

I'd barely sat down in my first period class when I was called to Hodson's office again.

This time Driscoll was there. "Mr. Hodson asked me to come. Told me about your antics here." No preliminaries. No how-are-you-doing stuff.

Cautiously, I sat down.

"You know you're walking on thin ice," he said.

I said, "I'm doing OK."

"Now that isn't what I've heard."

Hodson said, "I've checked with your teachers. You're failing everything but P.E."

I didn't bother to answer that. That wasn't why Driscoll was here.

Driscoll said, "Then there's the matter of the Walkman," getting to the point. "You can't deny you were there when it was taken. And it seems you have a motive too, something more than just seeing a nice Walkman and figuring you might as well pick it up. Mr. Hodson tells me it belongs to a kid who has a lot of influence in the school. He and his friends have been giving you a bad time. You knew what would happen if you got in a fight. Did you think you'd get away with this?"

"I'm not getting away with anything."

Hodson said, "You're damn right."

Driscoll said, "I've always thought you needed more supervision than this."

I'd heard that word before. All through the hearing Ms. Lloyd and Driscoll duking it out. Just how much "supervision" did I need? But Driscoll had lost.

"I was afraid your grandparents wouldn't be able to control you."

Control was a loaded word too.

I blurted out what Barry had said. "You can't prove I took it."

"Actually, it's more complicated than that."

"Complicated! Look, you've got to prove I did it—innocent until proven guilty and all—or you've got to leave me alone!"

Driscoll smiled. "I'm not about to leave you alone. Maybe no one has explained this to you, but you're already a ward of the court. For your previous crimes. That means the court is your parent, and, like a parent, gets to decide where you live. Your grandparents are caring for you, but for only as long as the court feels they are providing you with the care you need. If the court decides you need more supervision than they can provide, then it can assign you to a more supervised situation. Am I making myself clear?"

I felt myself go cold inside, as cold and gray as the view out the window behind Driscoll's head. Sure, I'd known this. But I hadn't thought of it that way.

"Besides, even if you didn't take it, you've violated the terms of your probation."

I just looked at him.

"Regular school attendance. That means going to school with books and paper and doing the work," he explained. "It means *passing* your classes."

"I thought . . ."

"I know what you thought. You thought you'd get away with anything you could. Don't think you're the first kid to think that. But you were wrong."

Why hadn't I known this? I could've done some of the schoolwork. Driscoll was probably planning to take me away right now. Make sure I got the "supervision" I needed. Why else would he have driven out here? Usually all he did was talk to me on the phone.

But he leaned back in his chair and said, "As you know, Ms. Lloyd doesn't agree with my assessment of your case. I figure I might as well give you a little more rope. Let's see if you can keep from hanging yourself."

So I got a reprieve.

Right away I started making a point of sitting up front in my classes and raising my hand any time I had a clue what the answer might be.

But I didn't even make it through the day.

I was headed to my last-period class. I stopped at my locker to get my math book as part of my new good student program. Mickey wasn't with me. She took a different math class, down at the other end of the hall. I was in the bonehead one, she was in the future scientists of America one, so we were never together at this time. The halls were full the way they always were between the periods, and I was aware of all the usual sounds of lockers slamming and people talking as I dug through my locker, wondering if my math book was really in there somewhere.

Then I felt a difference, a quiet. Slowly I turned around.

There was a ring of kids around me, standing back, leaving a good open space. Wyatt stood in the middle of that space. He said, "What you got in there?"

"What's it to you?"

"You don't happen to have a Walkman in there?"

I could see Trevor out in the ring. "Hey, Trevor. You always let this goon handle things for you?"

Trevor looked at me like he was above all this. But enjoying it, definitely enjoying it.

Wyatt said, "I do what I want."

"Right. As long as Trevor OK's it."

"You're scum," said Wyatt, and he spat on the floor.

"Yeah, scum," said someone else.

"We don't need scum like you around here." More than one kid said that.

This was looking serious. Only the week before I'd been one of the good guys who'd helped to fight the fire. Now I was a thief.

But I was determined not to hang myself. I figured I'd stall till the bell.

Except when the bell rang, not much else happened. Maybe a few on the outside wandered away, but most of the kids stayed. Eager to see me smashed into that wall of lockers, I guess.

Wyatt smiled. "Well, how about it, Alice?"

Then something changed again. The crowd shifted. Kids started moving away. In moments the hall was empty.

Except for me and Wyatt, and Jake.

"Go to class," Jake said to Wyatt. "I'll talk to you later about this."

It was over. Saved again. I took a deep breath

and unclenched my fists. But when I looked at Jake, I saw something was wrong. "I didn't start it," I said. How could he think I had?

"Come on in my office," he said.

This time the reprieve didn't last five minutes. Jake had to tell it to me twice, I found it so hard to believe.

"Now you think I stole a motorcycle?"

Jake pressed his fingers together. "I'm not saying that. Maybe it's just a coincidence. But Bruce thinks it might've been you."

I felt my stomach knot just at the mention of his name.

"Who else might've done it?" asked Jake.

"Anyone! A dirt bike? They're stolen all the time!"

"This one was stolen from your dad. Frankly, I've had a hard time believing you took the Walkman. I feel you're trying to make it here. And most of the time you're pretty clearheaded. But I can understand you not being so clearheaded about your dad."

"So I stole his motorcycle? How could I? I've never met him. I don't even know where he lives."

"Maybe it's time that changed."

"**D**o you need to get anything?" asked Jake.

"Huh?" Things were happening too fast for me.

"A jacket? Or maybe some schoolwork? After we go out to Bruce's place, I'll just take you home. So if you need anything for tonight . . ."

I finally understood what he was saying. "Yeah. I need some stuff from my locker."

"Then I'll meet you in the parking lot."

I still felt everything was whipping past me too fast, and I was stuck in slow motion, but I made my way to my locker, opened it, and stared into it for a while. Finally I managed to connect my brain back to my body enough to take out my jacket. But nothing else. The time for heroic studying had obviously passed. Then I went out the back door behind the gym.

I sure wasn't going to meet Jake in the parking lot.

Lately I'd been putting my dad into the dream. Only once in a while, but I'd do it. Now that I knew he

lived on a ranch, and had been a football player too, it
wasn't hard to imagine him looking like the guys in my
books. So I'd have him show up at just the right moment. When I was ambushed down in a canyon or
something. I'd hear these shots from the ridge behind
me. My enemies would start falling. When all the bad
guys had been wiped out, this tall stranger would come
down the hill and introduce himself as my dad. I'd
thank him for saving my life, and he'd tell me how much
he regretted all the years he'd been without me.

But even when I was making up that story in my
head, I knew it was wrong. Now this was all wrong.

There was no way I was going to convince him,
or Jake, or anyone, I hadn't taken his bike.

I kept the gym between me and the parking lot
and headed out across the wheat field behind the
school, not really thinking where I was going. But after
a while I found myself following the school bus route.

I was still cutting across the fields, not walking
along the road, but I saw the bus go by. I was glad I was
far enough away from the road the driver didn't get it
in his head to stop for me. I was also in no mood for
some friendly local to offer me a ride.

I just felt like walking. I didn't care that it was
still cloudy and cold. And kept getting darker and
colder. So that the fields that were green or golden only
yesterday now all looked gray. You could hardly see
where the sky ended and the ground began.

It felt good to be walking, with all that space around me. As long as I was walking, I didn't have to think what I was going to do next.

But when I came up over a ridge and could finally see my grandparents' place, the place I guess I'd been going to, I saw it was time to come up with some other plan.

A cop car was parked in the drive.

I thought about Barry's belief in truth while slipping behind the outbuildings, glad it had gotten so dark. I also thought about Driscoll, and I could almost see his face, hard and pale, the way it had looked when he came back from the phone.

I'd been picked up for panhandling, and my mom had turned me in as a runaway. The way she always did. Even though most of the time she acted like really her life would've been a whole lot better if I'd never been born, whenever I left, she'd call the police and tell them to bring me back. So they'd taken me to Detention. But it was no big deal. They'd call her. She'd come and get me. Complaining, of course, but she always came to get me. Anyway, that was what I was expecting. Driscoll must've expected that too. Until he made that call.

The truth hadn't mattered then, and it didn't now.

I saw the car was empty, so the cop was inside. I sure wasn't going to be there when he came out.

Maybe I could take the hay truck.

Right, car theft. You're really thinking now.

Instead I went into the garage, listening for any movement in the house. I opened the door of the pickup. Still no sound from the house. I got the flashlight out of the glove box. Then I leaned the seat forward because Grandma had said something about a blanket—now that winter was coming on someone ought to make sure the old blanket was still behind the seat of the truck. And it was. Last of all, I reached up to where the rifle hung across the back of the cab.

Was there anything else I should take?

Lately I'd been splitting wood for the woodstove almost every day. First Grandpa had let me do it all wrong, of course, and told me what an idiot I was. He'd never really told me how to do it. But somehow that had made it all the better when I'd finally figured out how to find the grain of the wood, how to swing the ax without holding the wood, fast and easy so it sank in with a satisfying whump. Then he'd noticed I was finally doing it right, and had said something. Short and simple, the way he did.

I found my eyes were stinging.

Cut it out. You're not going to cry.

Anyway, I took the small hatchet—Grandpa would need the ax—and left the garage, left everything, and started for the woods.

Sometimes I'd turn and look back at the house,

its windows yellow in the dark. Then I'd see the barred windows of Detention instead. The rolls of barbed wire at the top of the fence.

I'd turn and start walking again.

"Alex." For a moment I thought it was Grandma waking me for school. Then I felt the hard wood floor and remembered where I was.

"Alex."

I opened my eyes. "Mickey! How did you get here?"

"On Dufur. How'd you think? You don't sound happy to see me."

Of course I was happy to see her, but . . . I sat up and tried to pull myself awake.

"When you weren't at school today, and Hodson was asking everyone where you were, I knew I'd find you up here at the homestead."

"Did you tell him I was here?"

She sat down on the hearth, turned toward the fire I'd spent all night building, and started adding wood to it. It had burned down to coals, it needed the wood, but watching her poke at the fire like that, I saw it was her who wasn't so sure she wanted to see me.

"Well, *did* you?" I asked her. "Did you tell anyone you were coming here?"

She turned from the fire to face me. "That's all you want to know, isn't it? Did I tell someone. Is some-

one going to find you here. You took it, didn't you? It's
out there in one of those sheds. My mom was telling me
all these things, stuff she was hearing about you, and
she said if she'd known she never would've let me be
friends with you. I couldn't listen. I mean, I knew you
were different, and that was OK, I guess I kind of liked
that. But this . . . I told her it couldn't be true. But now
I see it *is* true."

I felt like all the air had been sucked out of the
room. I managed to say, "Go look for it out in the sheds
if you want."

Then I heard the roar of an engine. So she *had*
told someone. Or someone had followed her. But how
could someone have driven up here? Except . . .

I got up and went over to the windows, half surprised I could still do that. And, sure enough, there was
a motorcycle coming out of the woods. When the rider
swung off, and I saw it was Barry, I tried to come up
with some other explanation, but I couldn't. The bike
had to be my dad's. And Barry had done this to me.

I went out onto the porch thinking I should kill
him. Except it was still an effort just to breathe.

"Hey, Alex, how ya doing?" He slipped a backpack from his shoulders. "Brought you lots of food.
Thought you might be hungry."

I couldn't believe he was smiling at me. "You're
right, I'm hungry. I'm hiding up here with the cops after me. Thanks to you."

"Hey, you don't *have* to hide up here. But it's a great place to hide out, don't you think?"

He came up the steps, still smiling, like this was just about the neatest thing, and now we could all have a picnic around the fire.

Mickey stood in the doorway. She said, "Barry, how could you?"

"Hey, I just wanted to even things out. Like Robin Hood, you know. I mean, here's Alex with nothing. And then there's his dad, with just about everything. It's not a Kawasaki KX500, but it's great. Want to go for a ride?"

She said, "I'm not riding on any stolen motorcycle." But as mad as she was at him, she still kept her distance from me.

It wasn't like I hadn't expected this. Every day she had been with me.

"Forget the Robin Hood act," I said, my voice coming out as dead as I felt. "You had to know I'd be blamed for this. You set me up. It's as bad as whoever took the Walkman, doing it right when I was there."

He looked down. And I'd come to know that nervous look of his.

He'd taken the Walkman too!

And here I'd been maybe his only friend! I *was* going to kill him.

I came at him, and he backed up so quick he fell through the place where I'd torn up the railing and landed in a tangle of arms and legs and pieces of the porch. Then he jumped up fast and ran for the bike. Where I could've got him easily while he was madly kicking it, before it started up.

But I didn't bother, he looked so scared.

Everything was ruined anyway.

Mickey was scared of me too. She was on her horse almost as quick. And she never looked back.

17

The only good thing was Barry's backpack still sat on the porch. And I *was* hungry.

But after a while I got sick to my stomach. And not just from all the candy bars and chips. Even if Barry took that stuff back, told them what he'd done, Driscoll would say me running away showed I needed "more supervision." Besides, Grandpa had never wanted me here. Grandma had just talked him into it. There was no way I'd get to stay.

And Mickey wasn't going to let me near her again.

But in the morning I felt better. I looked around at where I was and saw Barry was right. If a guy was going to have to hide out, he couldn't ask for a better place. Not only was there a regular fireplace, so I didn't have to worry about burning down the forest, there was all that newspaper up in the attic, plus lots of wood just lying around at the edge of the meadow.

I decided if I couldn't make my life the way I wanted it to be, then I might as well try to live the dream. The guys in my books were always staying all alone out in places like this.

Sometimes they had a girlfriend, but never for long.

I went out and brought in a bunch more wood. Worked up a sweat chopping up the bigger pieces. That made me feel even more like the guys in my books. When I was thirsty, I just got a drink from the creek. I didn't worry about that beaver fever thing. 'Cause I really was like the pioneers now, taking my chances here. I scooped the water up in my hands, and it tasted just as good as I'd imagined it.

Then late in the afternoon, I heard something outside. You could hear everything there. It was one of the things I'd come to like about the place. I'd heard a deer that morning. Just some quiet footsteps, I'd looked out, and a deer had stood right by the porch. By the time I'd grabbed the rifle, it was gone, I couldn't find it anywhere. But there was no way Driscoll or the police could sneak up on me here.

Now I didn't think it was anyone like that. The sound was too quiet, more like the deer. Still, I kept to the side of the windows until I could see what it was. And I found it was Mickey! I rushed out to meet her. I couldn't believe she'd come back!

But she wasn't smiling as she slid off her horse, and she said, "I wasn't going to come."

I tried to recover, tried to keep my cool. "Love the greeting," I said.

"Well, I wasn't. Then I heard the weather report. It's going to snow tonight." When I didn't say anything, she repeated herself. "It's going to *snow* tonight."

"Right. That's what you said. I mean, that's neat. I've always wanted to see it snow. The places I've lived, well, sometimes it's snowed an inch or two, that's all."

She scowled at me. "Then you don't understand. You've got to get out of here."

"Why? People used to live up here. And I bet it used to snow."

"Well, they didn't just move here in November. They'd spend the whole summer getting ready for the winter. You don't even have boots!"

I looked down at my tennis shoes. I said, "I'm not going back."

"Look, I talked to Barry. He's pretty goofy. I mean, worse than I thought. I guess he's just been so lonely, he'd do anything to keep a friend. And we should've known he was into stealing. Nobody's parents ever gave them all that junk food. And Barry's parents, I mean, there's no way. But I think I've got him talked into . . ." She stopped, then looked up. "I'll tell you about it later. It's starting. We've got to go now."

I saw it was true that tiny white flakes were drifting down silently. Some of them sparkled in Mickey's hair. But she was still scowling, and holding tight to Dufur's reins. She hadn't changed her mind about me.

Nothing had changed.

I said, "I'm staying here. Sometimes I think this is where I was meant to be."

"What? You think you're like Romeo or something?"

That threw me. I said, "Romeo?"

"That's what you're saying. You're saying it's your fate to stay up here and freeze to death."

"Hey, you know I haven't been following that Romeo and Juliet stuff. But maybe there is something like fate. I mean, I was trying to make things work out."

She looked at me even more furiously. "Well, maybe you should've paid more attention in that class. 'Cause we talked about that a lot. And Romeo was wrong about that star-crossed stuff. He didn't have to kill himself. And you're wrong too. You think it's supposed to be easy? I want to make some kind of career with my art. You think that's going to be easy? You think it's going to be easy to even convince my parents to let me try?"

Sometimes Mickey could talk awfully fast. First she'd dragged in Shakespeare, and now her drawing? All I could think to say was, "Please don't tell anyone where I am. You know I didn't take that stuff."

"Alex, don't you see what you're doing to me?"

No, I didn't see. And now she had me even more

confused, almost tricking myself into thinking she still liked me.

But then her voice got really quiet and cold, and she said, "I guess I knew you'd say something dumb like that. So I brought you all the food I could. 'Cause we always go to Pendleton, to my grandmother's, for Thanksgiving. We'll be gone all weekend. But Alex, if it snows a lot, and they say it might, I won't be able to get up here again. If it does that, promise me you'll walk out. Promise me you won't do anything stupid."

I looked at her, still confused, by what she was saying, and what she wasn't saying too. But I reminded myself the guys in my books never got close to anyone.

"I don't think I can promise not to do anything stupid," I said.

When I woke the next morning, I found the world had turned completely white. I went out onto the porch and couldn't believe how beautiful it was. Smooth white curves covered the ground. Puffs of white hung from the trees. It looked like a Christmas card.

I waded through the snow down to the creek, even though Mickey was right about my shoes not working too great for that, and the water of the creek was crystal cold, the best I'd ever drunk. Then I beat down a path as I carried in more wood. The snow had covered the wood on the ground, but the lower branches of the trees were dead and easy to chop off. I found they burned good too. It made me feel pretty smart to figure that out, and working like that really warmed me up.

But it also got me thinking about the way I'd worked with Grandpa. With the old guy always badgering me, but liking me too.

At least that was what I'd thought.

It doesn't matter. You don't need Grandpa, or anyone.

I put my shoes by the fire to dry. My jeans were wet from the knees down, so I took them off too.

See, you couldn't do that if somebody else was here. It's going to be good to be all alone.

Then I spread out all my food.

I had kind of looked forward to going out hunting, but so far I hadn't had to. I still had a huge stack of ham and cheese sandwiches from what Mickey had brought, some apples, plus another bag of chips and a couple of candy bars from Barry's backpack. I started on one of the sandwiches, thinking it looked like some kind of feast.

But that made me remember it was Thanksgiving. And Mickey was making a big deal of it with her family.

All it had ever been for me was a vacation from school. The only kind of turkey my mom ever cooked came in a box.

Then I realized Grandma would've done a Thanksgiving dinner for me this time, with the dressing and the pumpkin pie and all, just like you see on TV.

Forget it. You would've spent the day in Detention, waiting to go to MacBride.

You should be thankful you're here.

For lunch, more ham and cheese sandwiches, an

apple, and a candy bar. For dinner, even more sandwiches and a bag of chips. I was glad I didn't have to
go out hunting, 'cause the snow was still coming down.
But inside it was warm. I liked watching the fire lick
around the wood. I took out my knife — glad Grandpa
had finally given it back to me — and tried to figure out
what "whittling" was, until even leaning close to the
fire it was too dark to see.

The next morning it was still snowing hard. But I just
went out onto the porch and peed. Another benefit of
being alone. Then I got myself a handful of snow instead of walking down to the creek — never eat yellow
snow. I picked up the broken pieces of the railing —
they'd come in handy as firewood now — and went
back into the warmth of the house.

    I was beginning to run low on food. I had only
two sandwiches left, one for breakfast and one for
lunch. Then for dinner my last apple and a bag of chips,
and I licked all the wrappers for dessert. But I knew I
could go for a while without eating, as long as I had water. And I did. I had all that snow and the creek. As
soon as it stopped snowing, I'd go find that deer. Then
I'd have plenty of food.

    I went out onto the porch one last time, watched
the snow swirl down through the darkness, then went
back in to sleep.

———

Bright sunlight woke me. I looked at it shining through the windows and was glad. I'd enjoyed the snow, but I was ready for it to melt.

But when I went out, I found if anything it was colder than it had been. I could feel the cold all the way down into my lungs. The snow sparkled in the sunlight, but it didn't look like it had melted at all.

I stood there eating handfuls of it, then realized that wasn't enough. I was still thirsty, so I stepped off the porch—and fell in! It was a whole lot deeper than I'd expected, almost up to my waist.

I finally managed to stand myself up, then I shoved my way through the stuff. At least the creek wasn't very far. But when I got to the creek, or where the creek should've been, I couldn't find it. I dug through the snow until my hands turned red with the cold, but I couldn't find the water anywhere. I couldn't hear it either, bubbling the way it always did.

Then it came to me the creek was frozen.

I shivered in the blanket while all my clothes lay drying by the fire. For the first time I wondered if I should walk out. I never thought it would snow this much.

I never imagined the creek could freeze.

Calm down. You're getting warm. Your clothes are getting dry. The creek will thaw. The snow will melt. Maybe it'll take a day or so, but with the sun that bright, it's bound to warm up. You don't want to try to walk out in this.

Think about something else.

Maybe I could really carve something. That would give me something to do. First I picked out a piece of wood. I knew I shouldn't try anything too hard, but I thought I could maybe make a cat curled up in a ball with its nose tucked under its paw. It would've been nice to have a cat with me now, a warm cat purring on my lap.

And as I tried to get the curve of its back and the shape of the head with its pointed ears, it did get my mind off the frozen creek. Instead I was thinking of all the cats I'd had. The skinny orange one who'd had kittens on my bed. The black one who'd looked like a panther. The one that had made a pile of dead mice in a corner of my room.

I'd always liked cats, and as soon as we'd move into a new place, the cats in the area seemed to know. One would wander in, and my mom would let me keep it. She said she liked cats too. Even if the landlord had said no pets, we'd always have a cat. It would be our secret. My mom and I hiding this cat.

But when she decided to move again, she never took the cats with us. "That scruffy old thing! It's mooched off us long enough." Sometimes I'd beg her to keep one of them, but I learned not to. She'd say, "Stop your whining," pick up the cat and toss it out the door. It'd go flying, legs outstretched, scared, twisting to land upright.

The same cat she'd cuddled under her chin and talked to in baby talk.

I found myself trying to saw the head off the cat. So I threw it in the fire and watched it burn.

That night I woke in a panic, in a sweat. Crazy dreams, fever dreams. Almost as bad as the nightmares I used to have when I was a little kid that would bring me awake like this, and my room would be completely changed. My shirt on the floor would've become a monster crawling toward me. The blinking light across the street a spaceship full of more monsters. I'd run for my mom's room and crawl into the warmth of her bed. She'd wrap herself around me. "Alex, it's all right."

But sometimes instead of it being like that, the man beside her would growl something, and she'd yell at me, "Haven't I told you never to come into my bedroom in the night!"

Now I lay there in the dark and felt the way I would when I had to go back to my room. Alone. With the spaceship still at the window and the monster still on the floor.

You wanted to be alone, remember. Just like the guys in your books.

The next morning it was still sunny, but also still cold. How could it be so sunny and cold? I felt dizzy. Maybe I really had caught some kind of flu in the night.

I knew I needed to get more wood. The stack by the fireplace was almost gone. So I pulled up the rest of the porch railing. I couldn't make myself go out again into that waist-deep snow.

Maybe if I got something to eat, that would make me feel better. So I brought the rifle out onto the porch, to be ready the next time that deer wandered by. I aimed it at a nearby tree, just to try it out and see what I could hit, pulled the trigger—and there was only a quiet click.

My stomach immediately let me know what it thought of that. I'd counted on the rifle. I'd never thought to see if it was loaded.

All I could think to do then was to eat more snow. Even though I could tell it didn't do much good, for either my hunger or my thirst. Then I went back in and lay by the fire. I watched the cobwebs dangling from the ceiling sway in the draft, and every once in a while I tossed on another stick of wood.

Until there was no more left.

I knew I had to walk out.

But could I walk out now?

Think about the guys you've read about. This snow wouldn't bother them. They crossed mountain passes in snow that was deeper than this.

In tennis shoes?

In moccasins. Barefoot. Didn't one of them crawl fifty miles on his hands and knees with his scalp ripped off?

But all that hero-dream stuff was very far away.

Detention and Driscoll also seemed very far away. There was just me, way up in the woods, in maybe four feet of snow.

I didn't want to be alone anymore.

I still felt like I might be sick. My head ached, and what was going on in my stomach wasn't just emptiness. But I put on my jacket and forced myself to go out onto the porch again. There I scooped up a huge handful of snow and let it melt in my mouth. It made my lips and my mouth feel better, but it melted into nothing. A trickle of water. No wonder it didn't quench my thirst. Then I started pushing my way through all that snow.

Soon my hands and feet were screaming with the cold. Well, I didn't have boots. Or gloves either. After a while, my hands and feet weren't just cold, they got stiff, like hunks of concrete. Hunks of concrete that hurt. My throat was so dry, it hurt too with each breath. But inside the jacket I was sweating. Pretty strange, I thought.

So many things were strange. That I could be both cold and hot. I was also both happy and sad. Sad I was leaving the homestead. Sad I was going back to whatever Driscoll might do to me. But happy I was going to see Grandma and Grandpa again, even if they didn't want me. And Mickey too. Maybe if I walked out, maybe if I talked to her, she'd at least be a friend.

Did my heroes ever miss the people they'd left?

I kept shoving my way through that snow until I made it up to the ridge. But then I had to rest. I'd gotten so hot inside the jacket I didn't think it would hurt to lie down. I'd read about people dying because they fell asleep, so I wouldn't lie down very long. But the snow was so soft, like a big white pillow, and the sun was so bright that I closed my eyes. . . .

I started shivering all over. My teeth were chattering. I pushed myself up and turned dizzily in the sun, blinded by it shining on the snow, and at first not knowing where I was.

Then I found I could see the mountain, and I knew I should keep it on my left. So I made myself start moving again. But each time I saw the mountain, the sun was hanging closer to it. Until the south side of the mountain was golden. Then when I saw it, it was orange. The next time, the mountain was pink, and the sun was gone.

Now the sky was lit by the sunset. The snow turned an icy blue. And I was still high up on the ridge. Still a long way from my grandparents' place. Why hadn't I started walking first thing in the morning?

I felt I had to rest again. My throat hurt. My lungs hurt. My hands hurt. I had to rest. But only for a moment, I told myself.

Then I was up again, plunging on again. But now I was stumbling and falling, and each time I almost cried to have to put my hands in the snow to push myself back up. I thought this must be the way you feel when you're drowning, and you're kicking and kicking, but your head keeps sinking below the water.

The sky was turning black. I felt what little heat there was was being sucked up into that blackness.

You've got to keep moving. Keep moving.

But I fell again. Powdery white crystals so close to my face.

How could I have forgotten that nothing I tried worked out. Ms. Lloyd shouldn't have bothered doing anything for me.

The stars were now coming out, a whole dome of them arching over my head.

Star-crossed, I thought.

And I was coming home to my mother's house for the last time. The very last time. But I didn't know that yet. I was opening the door, and the scene was gruesome, but no worse than other homecomings. She'd been lying on the couch, but she pulled herself up, gathered all her strength just to yell at me. About what? I couldn't remember.

The snow was so soft, the stars so wonderfully bright.

But I could remember the red that was spreading across her face, beginning to turn black. Already one of her eyes was black. She was wearing just a flimsy robe of some kind, and I could see through it. I could see she was pretty banged up, and bent over, clutching her stomach. But not so hurt she couldn't yell at me.

I yelled back at her. "Why do you always have these scumbags in your life?"

"Don't talk to me like that."

"You think they love you when they treat you like this? You make me want to puke."

"It's nothing. You're the problem here. You never think of anyone but yourself. Out at all hours of the night. In trouble all the time."

And she hit me. I could still feel it. The sting on my cheek, quick and hard.

It had been a long time since she'd been able to do much to me. She'd just slap me across the face like that. Just a slap. It didn't really hurt.

But it did hurt. And it hurt to see her like that. This time I hit her back.

"There. See, I can do it too. Guess that makes me a man."

Then she was chasing me. I was running too. I was running away again.

Got to get up. Got to keep moving. But I was no longer cold.

Brutally beaten. Internal bleeding. Had to be hospitalized.

My thoughts were hazy and far away like the stars.

"She's lying. I only hit her once."

"Were you drunk? Were you on drugs?"

It was so quiet and soft and warm.

Driscoll coming back from the phone. "Your mother. Your own mother. If I had my way, you would spend years behind bars."

Then it wasn't so quiet. Or maybe that was just another memory. I was with my friends down at the railroad tracks. "Bet you can't lie on the tracks." "When's the next train?" "You're not scared, are you?" "No, I'm not scared." Never scared, I thought. I'm tough, like the men in those books. Then the rumbling sound. The headlight coming at me.

More headlights coming, lighting up the night.

"There's something over there in the snow."

"What is it, Bruce?"

"I think it's him."

A man was leaning down close to me, then picking me up in his arms.

The attic room. I knew that was where I was. With the white ceiling angling down. But I looked up through a long tunnel at it, at the room and the faces that would lean over me. Grandma's face. Mickey's. Also the man who'd come with the headlights and the rumbling sound. I felt I remembered his face from a very old dream.

But I didn't see Grandpa. I thought he must be awfully mad at me.

After a while the tunnel got shorter. I could feel my body around me again. No one was there just then. Sunlight streamed in through the window, and I watched the dust swirl in the light.

Then Mickey's mother came in. That seemed odd. She said, "Oh, I see you're finally awake."

"Where's Grandma and Grandpa?" I asked.

She just left saying she'd get me something to eat. But before she got back, I must've fallen back to sleep.

When I woke again, Mickey was there. She immediately started coming down on me for not walking out sooner, and what was I trying to do? Still, I was glad to see her. And she brought me soup with huge chunks of chicken in it, and celery, and wide noodles, and Grandma's green beans. It felt good all the way down.

I said, "Grandma sure makes good soup."

Mickey said, "I made it."

"I'm impressed. I didn't know . . ."

"I could cook?"

"Well, I didn't think it was the kind that came from a can. And I thought they were Grandma's green beans."

"It sure didn't come from a can. You're just making things worse, you know."

Then she grinned, and I felt it. It was a lot like the soup, the way it warmed me all the way through.

It gave me the courage to say, "Not all the stories you heard about me are true. The one about my mom, well, it's only partly true."

She said, "I didn't hear one about your mom. But I thought about it, I thought about you, and . . . Hey, you think I'd go to all this work for someone I didn't like? I put that chicken on the stove this morning, before I left for school."

"Thanks." Now I was grinning too. "It's the best soup I've ever had."

"But you're right that the green beans are Effie's. It's her recipe too. So I guess I should forgive you, but right now she's too busy to be making you soup."

Then her grin disappeared.

I felt that too, like a chill. "Why is Grandma so busy?"

Mickey looked away. "She'll be home pretty soon." She straightened the table beside the bed. It didn't need straightening.

"Where is she?" Then, when Mickey still didn't answer, "What's wrong?" And finally, as the idea came to me, "Where's Grandpa?"

"Alex, I'm sorry. I'm not supposed to say anything."

"You've got to tell me now!"

"I just don't know much," she insisted. "But I think he's going to be all right."

"You think?" I almost dropped the soup all over the bed.

"Effie should be home really soon. She'll be able to tell you everything. Except she said she didn't want you to know. I'm not sure why. She just wanted you to rest. But . . . well . . ."

"Grandpa had a heart attack."

I could tell by her face I'd guessed right. But Mickey wouldn't say anything more, no matter how much I begged her to tell me how bad it was. Then when we finally heard Grandma in the drive, she said, "I'll go tell her you know," and hurried away.

Next I heard the two of them in the kitchen, opening and closing the refrigerator door, opening and closing the outside door. How could they be unloading groceries now? I swung my legs over the side of the bed. I had to find out how Grandpa was! But when I tried to stand up, a wave of blackness closed across my eyes. I had to lie back down.

Finally Grandma came up the stairs. I watched her come into the room, and I could see how tired she was. But she smiled when she sat down on the bed. "I'm glad to see you're awake. The doctor said you were going to be all right, but I couldn't help worrying. And you've eaten something too. That's good. How are you feeling?"

"I'm OK. How's Grandpa?"

She smiled again, but now there was a sadness to it. "He's doing a lot better today. They took him out of intensive care. He's going to be just fine."

That sounded good. But even though I didn't know much about heart attacks, I didn't think getting over one was like getting over a flu.

"How did it happen?"

At that she frowned. "It was the snow. And the cold. And . . ." Her lips drew together into a tight line. She forced them into another thin smile. "What's important is he's going to be all right. And you're going to be all right too."

I felt there was something she wasn't saying. I asked her again, "How'd it happen?"

"Alex." She put her hand over mine where it lay on the quilt. It felt funny, not something she'd ever done before. "I don't want you to feel bad about this," she said.

"Bad about what?" I was scared again.

"Well, you left. We didn't know where you'd gone. We were so worried. Then it snowed."

"He went out looking for me?"

"He tried, but he didn't get far. Thank God. And it didn't knock him down. It wasn't that kind of thing. He felt it, and he was able to get back to the house. He knew exactly what it was."

"He went out looking for me?" I said it again because I couldn't believe it. Grandma must've made him go look for me.

But she said, "He was so afraid you were lost in the snow. And he blamed himself, for what he'd said. He gets angry like that, and he says things without thinking. He knows he does it. Then he feels bad." She looked down. "I know he feels bad about Linda too. I guess he can't forgive her now, but he didn't want to be like that with you."

She looked back up at me. "He likes to say it was my idea to have you come here. But really, it was his. After Ms. Lloyd called us, all he could talk about was you and what fun it had been when you stayed with us that summer. And this time, he's enjoyed working with you so much. Every day he tells me all about everything you've been learning. He's been so proud of you."

She'd said she didn't want me to feel bad. She

shouldn't have worried. I didn't feel bad. At least not then. Later I realized how I'd hurt Grandpa. And Grandma too. But right then all I felt was more of the warmth. Like the soup. Like Mickey's grin.

Grandpa had cared so much about me, he'd gone out into the snow to find me, knowing it wasn't good for his heart.

I was still getting that into my head, seeing how it changed everything I'd thought before, when I heard a pickup drive in. By then it was evening, Mickey'd gone home, saying her mom didn't want her spending much time with me, but I was still feeling good about her too. And I'd had a lot more soup. Then I heard a man's voice talking to Grandma, next footsteps on the stairs.

Grandma appeared in the doorway. "Alex, are you awake?" She looked hesitant, maybe even scared. It made me suddenly alert. I could barely see the shadow of the man behind her. But Driscoll wouldn't drive out here in a pickup. Could it be the police?

Then she stepped to the side to let him come in. "Your father is here to see you."

There stood the man who'd found me in the snow. He said, "How you feeling?"

I managed to croak out, "OK."

Grandma came over and started propping up the pillows. Which was good. I sure didn't want to do this flat on my back.

"The snow here can get serious. Not something to mess with," he said.

"Yeah. Guess I learned that." Then added quickly, "Thanks for finding me."

'Cause I knew he'd saved my life. I got this flip-flopping in my chest. It was like the dream had come true. He even looked like the heroes of my books. A tall man in faded jeans and a shirt with that fancy cowboy trim. Everything but the hat and the guns.

He took another step into the room and looked around, probably for a chair. But there wasn't one. He said, "Mind if I sit on the bed?"

"Sure. I mean, no. Go ahead."

So he sat down, but with his legs braced like he didn't want to put too much weight on the bed. Grandma had finished with the pillows. She said, "Maybe I should leave you alone." Then there was just the two of us, looking at each other.

He said, "You must hate me."

"No." It came out quick. But I didn't think I hated him.

"You have plenty of reason to. But your mother, she was so mad at me, she didn't want me to see you at all. For a while I tried. I even followed the two of you. I didn't want to lose you."

So that part was true.

"But then, my family was asking me to come back here, help out with the ranch. And Linda, it got so

I couldn't stand to even talk to her on the phone. And I couldn't see you without talking to her. Guess I gave up. But I'll be able to see you now. We'll go out on the snowmobiles, OK?"

"That'd be great!" I pulled myself up a little straighter, and I said, "I do look like you. Hodson said that. That I looked like you. I didn't know."

He kind of laughed and said, "Hodson, bet he's still mad at me for not taking one of those scholarships."

"Yeah, he is," and I kind of laughed too. I couldn't believe this was happening. It *was* just like the dream.

Then he rubbed his hands on his jeans and said, "Look, Alex, I'm really glad I came to see you. I should've done it earlier, I know. But I don't want you to misunderstand. I don't want you to be disappointed."

I hurried to tell him, "Hey, I know you're married. And have other kids."

"That's right. And Cheryl and I have talked a lot about this, about you." He rubbed his hands on his jeans some more. "That's why I should probably tell you now. Cheryl, my wife, well, she's concerned. She understands that I want to see you, but she doesn't want you at the house."

"Sure, I mean I never thought I'd live with you. I like it here."

"No, it's more than that."

He was looking at the wall now, not me. But I

was studying every inch of him, and beginning to think he wasn't that much like the guys in my books. They never hedged around like this. What was he getting at?

He said, "She doesn't think it would be a good idea to have you around the kids."

The flip-flopping in my chest did a complete somersault. "Right. I wouldn't want to corrupt *your* kids."

"It's just that Jenny, she's almost twelve."

"Hey, I get it."

"But we'll go out on the snowmobiles, like I said. I know you'll like them."

And I was sure I would. Now my insides were flipping all around. This guy was still my dad, and I could remember a little of the night before, the speed and the spray of snow.

Then he said, "They're kind of like *motorcycles*, you know," watching me closely when he said "motorcycles," and I realized he still thought I'd taken his bike.

"I bet they are." I looked him right in the eye. "But then I've never ridden on a motorcycle."

You could tell he didn't believe me. And at first I thought, you can't blame him for that. I started to explain about Barry. Then I stopped myself.

'Cause it hit me he was the one who was lying. All that stuff about my mom being such a pain, and how he had to come back here to the ranch. He could've seen me. If he'd wanted to. Maybe now he was mad about the bike, but that didn't explain the whole thirteen years of me not knowing him at all, not getting even a card from him. And I'd been in Rimrock for over a month. Except that Cheryl, well, she was "concerned."

I felt like an idiot for saying that thing about us looking alike.

He said, "I guess I shouldn't stay very long. I don't want to wear you out. But I'm glad Effie called me. Glad she remembered I had snowmobiles and all."

Or he might've never come to see me.

He said some more about how he was pleased I was feeling so good. But all the time he was saying that stuff, I figured he was wondering where I'd left his bike buried up in the snow, and thinking up ways to protect "the kids" from me. The only thing he'd said straight was that I had plenty of reasons to hate him.

You'd think I would've learned not to trust my dreams.

Still, before he left, I thanked him again for going out into the snow and finding me, and bringing me back here, keeping my voice as flat as I could make it. 'Cause I really was glad he'd done that.

21

But was there any way I could stay here? I realized I had to prove I wasn't the local thief.

Grandma insisted I rest the next day, and she spent most of it at the hospital, but that evening I told her I was ready to go back to school. She frowned and said she thought I should stay home another day.

I said, "I'm feeling good."

She went over to the sink and kind of stared out the window. I thought she must be thinking about Grandpa. Then she said, "Tomorrow I have to go to a meeting at the school. Maybe you should just wait here."

"No! I've got to go to school!" I could tell by her voice exactly what kind of meeting it was going to be.

"Well, I guess, if you want to," she said.

I snagged Barry as soon as he got on the bus. When he saw me, he began to back down the steps. But I pulled him into a seat by me and Mickey and said, "You've got to help me straighten this out. You've got to take that stuff back. And tell them it was you, not me."

"Hey, I can't. I mean, I really didn't want to mess things up for you. But I can't."

"Yes, you can. They won't do anything to you like what they'll do to me."

"How do you know?"

"Believe me, I know. You've never been in trouble before, right?"

Barry squirmed away from me.

"They always give kids lots of chances. You take the stuff back, tell them you're sorry. Maybe they'll give you some community service. But they're past giving me any more chances."

"I'm going to tell them," said Mickey, "whether you do or not. It'll look better if you do it."

"OK. OK. You guys win."

So I dragged him into Hodson's office first thing. I didn't give him a chance to disappear on me. And Barry did a good job. You could tell it wasn't easy for him, but he stood there and explained it all, then waited for whatever was going to hit him. Made me remember why'd I'd come to like the guy. Maybe with his goofy logic taking that stuff did make sense.

But Hodson just nodded and said, "Well, Barry, looks like you need to talk to the police." And the way he looked at me you could tell he still felt he had me neatly cupped in his hand, and later that day he'd get to toss me around his office a little, see how I bounced.

Between each class I checked the parking lot to see if Grandma was there yet. Mickey misunderstood the way I went outside on every break. She said, "A lot of the kids are feeling bad about the way they treated you. Trevor told me he was feeling bad. Maybe Wyatt will still be a jerk, but things are going to be OK."

I was glad to hear all that, but it didn't help. Then just before fifth period I saw Grandma's pickup. Driscoll's car was there too. It was just a plain green car with government plates, but I knew it was Driscoll's.

We were on our way to English class, but I stopped at Hodson's office. Mickey noticed she'd lost me and came back. "Hey, come on."

I said, "I'm not going to class." There was no way I could sit through a class knowing Driscoll was meeting with Grandma and Hodson.

"Alex, what's wrong?"

The bell rang. It was deafening there by the offices.

"Just go on," I told her. "You're going to be late."

She looked at me almost the way she had when I told her I was going to stay at the homestead. But she did finally leave me there. Staring at Hodson's door and wishing I had X-ray vision. Everyone else disappeared into the classrooms.

Then Jake was at my side.

"So they didn't invite you to the meeting either," I said.

"Nothing's been decided yet. You can wait in my office if you want."

"No thanks."

"I've got some paperwork to do. We don't have to talk."

"I didn't take the stuff. Barry did."

"Yes, we know, but you ran away."

I knew they were going to hold that against me. "But I was being blamed for something I didn't do. Anyone would run away from that. I came back."

"And you took a gun."

That stopped me. "But I didn't . . ."

"We know what you didn't do. It's the things you did do that count. And now your grandfather is ill."

"That's why I need to stay here!" I finally turned to face him. "Grandma and Grandpa are going to need my help. Even more than before."

"I really wish you'd come in and sit down. They could be in there a long time."

"But isn't that true? Grandpa's going to need me now."

"Yes, I guess you're right. But, well . . ." His voice dropped. "There's also the matter of the fire."

I could only stare at him.

"Arson is a serious count."

When I was finally able to speak, I thought I sounded like a little kid. "I didn't do it on purpose."

"Maybe. Maybe not. Your grandmother told me about it just because she was telling me everything, trying to figure out what to do. And she thought it was probably an accident. She wasn't even sure you had done it. On the other hand, your mother came to see you that night. You got pretty upset. And you know, you don't think clearly when you're upset. The first time I saw you, you were starting to light a fire on my desk. Now will you come in my office?"

I backed away from him.

"Don't try to run," said Jake.

Funny, for once I wasn't even thinking of running away.

"I'll be right outside," I said.

I turned and headed for the double doors. What was going on? I finally figure things out. At least I'd figured a lot of things out. I knew who I wanted to be. Not the lone hero riding off into the sunset, but just a guy with friends and a family. And I'd found my friends and my family here!

Not my dad, for sure. And not my mom either.

But people I wanted to stay with. Now I wasn't going to get to show anyone what I'd learned.

Then I saw Wyatt coming toward me. Wyatt was outside. Probably he'd been doing something for the coach. He was always getting out of class to do things for the coach. He yanked open the door I was leaning on, and he grinned, his shoulder only inches from my chest. "Hey, some trick getting Barry to take the rap."

His face was also just inches away. And that

grin. Right there in front of the offices. With the secretary right behind the glass. And Jake watching too. Jake had started for his office, but he'd stopped by his door to watch.

It was perfect. For Wyatt. Just more of his good clean fun. "So the jailbird gets to fly free a little longer," he said.

But it was perfect for me too.

He didn't even know how right he was, how I wasn't going to be "flying free" for more than another hour, if that. And sure enough, he wasn't expecting anything. I was able to bury my fist in his stomach. He didn't recover too swiftly either. I'd planted a couple of good ones right in his face before the guy got himself in gear. By then I had him backed right into those doors. He was big, he was angry. But I was angry too. At everything and everyone.

If it was my fate to lose, then I'd do it with blood on my fists.

I was only vaguely aware of other people. Yelling. Someone grabbing me from behind. Jake. I turned and fought him off, turned back to Wyatt again.

Then someone else came up behind me, kicked my knees out from under me. And I found I had only one hand to catch myself. Someone had the other one. I felt the handcuff close.

I tried to roll over to face Driscoll, to strike out at him with my free arm, but he was on top of me, one knee hard in my back, pulling the handcuffed hand up behind me. Then he had both my wrists.

He pulled me up by the arms, and there was Grandma looking at me. Just looking at me. I swayed on my feet, with Driscoll's grip maybe the only thing keeping me upright. I couldn't meet her eyes.

"Why?" she said finally. As if I could explain it.

Driscoll explained it instead. "I told you something like this was likely to happen. You did the best you could."

22

I figured that was the end. As I rode in the back of Driscoll's car, with a chain around my waist, my hands cuffed, my legs in shackles, there was no doubt in my mind.

But I guess as long as you don't die, it's not the end.

Still, I never expected Grandma to show up at MacBride.

It was a Sunday, and I knew visiting time was close. You could feel it, the way some of the kids were edgy, either because they expected someone or knew someone wouldn't come. But I was just reading a book, practicing my sitting. Basically you had two choices there. You could get Mace squirted in your eyes and be hauled away to this cell block they liked to call the Crisis Intervention Unit. Or you could learn how to sit.

Of course, you also got to march two by two from one building to another, and once in a while you'd get to go outside and toss a ball around, with security cars parked at all the places you might run. Otherwise, the rule was you could move from one chair to another. But no standing around, something I now realized I used to do all the time.

And it was only the sitting time that counted. You couldn't just mark the calendar and say this is when I get out. Driscoll had said he'd be glad to keep me there until I was twenty-one. Or I could get out a lot sooner by gluing myself to a chair.

So that was what I was doing when a staff guy called my name.

Next I found myself still sitting, but facing Grandma in this room where they usually served us our meals. Rows of tables just like the one we were at, with little groups of people scattered here and there, each centered around a kid in jeans and T-shirt exactly like mine. But even though there were all those people in that room, there was hardly any noise. Only a few little sisters and brothers were acting halfway normal, running around under the tables and breaking the quiet sometimes with a shriek or a laugh.

Grandma said, "How are you doing?" and her voice was quiet too.

I said, "All right, I guess. How's Grandpa?" my voice as low as hers.

"He's doing good. He's home from the hospital, and every day he gets stronger."

We talked like that, and I think all the conversations in that room must've sounded like that. Everyone stiff and cautious. Trying not to say anything that would admit they were really here, where none of the windows opened and the doors were always locked.

Then Grandma broke through all that playacting. "Alex, why did you do that to Wyatt?"

And she waited. She didn't let me off the hook.

And Driscoll wasn't there to answer for me.

Finally I said, "What difference does it make?"

She still refused to fill in the silence with the careful talk everyone else was using to avoid this kind of thing.

"Look," I said, "I know I lost it. But it doesn't matter. I wasn't going to get to stay there anyway."

Her eyes got very sad then. "Alex, I want you to know this. Before you did that, I'd convinced Mr. Driscoll to let you stay with us."

I felt numb.

"So why did you do it?" Her eyes studied mine. You could see she really wanted to know.

But I didn't know. After a while I said that. "I don't know. I guess I gave up."

That night, when I found myself again trying to sleep on this bed that was too short for me, locked in this room with twenty-four other kids, with the lights on—they never dared turn off the lights—I could still hear myself saying that. I could hear the echo too, my dad saying the same thing.

And I saw even though a lot had gone wrong—

Mickey was right that things weren't easy, not easy at all—things sure hadn't been easy for me—still, me being here at MacBride had nothing to do with fate. And maybe Romeo wasn't a jerk. Sometimes it's awfully hard to see you have a choice.

But it still wasn't the end.

Grandma kept coming to see me. She couldn't make the drive every week, but almost every other week she'd come, and we'd talk about Grandpa and Mickey, and the weather and the ranch. Then, every once in a while, she'd say something again. Something that would leave me going over and over it long after she was gone.

One time she really did it.

First she took a deep breath so you could tell she was going to dive down deep. Then she said, "Alex, I want you to know I never believed Linda's story. Even when she was a little girl, she would tell lies. And when she talked to me about it on the phone, she told me how the police, when she had to go to the hospital, insisted she press charges. Kept badgering her till she did. I think she decided to name you because she was afraid of the man who had really done it. Or maybe she still loved him."

And Grandma didn't quit with that.

She said, "I wanted to believe her. I've always tried to believe her. It's been hard for me to really blame her for the things she's done. It's been easier to blame myself. And Leland. And pretend she didn't do some of the worse things. It's so hard to know someone you love has done such terrible things. Maybe I should have tried to take you from her, but I couldn't see that then."

I was still back on that stuff about the police and the hospital. But Grandma wasn't going to stop to let me catch up.

She said, "I know Leland and I made mistakes, and I wish I could undo some of them, but now I realize we didn't make her get pregnant so young, we didn't make her marriage fail, or make it so she couldn't keep a job." Then she really surprised me by saying, "Sometimes I think you're still believing her too. We've both got to stop believing her, Alex. We both want to help her. But believing her isn't helping her."

I got the feeling Grandma was lying awake thinking all night just like me.

That night I just kept running through everything she'd said. And at first I thought, she's crazy. Don't I know I can't believe my mom?

Then I found myself remembering the other times.

When my mom would ask me to forgive her. She'd never meant to hurt me. "Come hold me," she'd say. She always put it that way, ask me to hold her instead of saying it the other way around. And even when I was so small I'd be sitting in her lap, I'd feel it was me holding her.

'Cause I was tough. And she seemed so fragile. I'd ask her to please forgive *me*. I knew I'd made her do it. You could tell she loved me. She'd never hurt me if I wasn't always doing things wrong.

And sometimes she'd come into my room — she still did this, had done it only a few months ago — and she'd sit on my bed and just talk and talk. I knew it was only when she was between boyfriends, and was sober too. But she was between boyfriends a lot.

Anyway, she'd be quiet then. Not bubbly and smiley the way she was when she was telling her lies. Not angry and shrill either. Just quiet. Honest. As honest as she knew how to be. And she'd talk to me about all kinds of things. Lots of stuff I could barely understand, especially when I was younger.

How she wished she could figure out why she kept making the same mistakes.

As I got older, sure, I'd heard it all before. But at times like that, I'd still listen. It felt good to have her sitting there on my bed, just the two of us quiet in my room. 'Cause right then, with her talking like that, I knew I was the only person she had.

Really, it was something I always knew. Even when I ran away and stayed away for days. Sure, sometimes the cops would pick me up before I was ready to go home. But most of the time they didn't. Still, I always went back. And it wasn't for the package of green bologna in the refrigerator.

She needed me. Those guys didn't really care about her.

And she knew that too. During those quiet, honest times, she'd say it. "Alex, what would I do without you? Without you I'd be just like those leaves blowing around in the breeze. You know that, don't you? No matter what else I say?"

Now I saw she'd been the only person I had too. For all those years, in all those towns. No wonder I'd been willing to listen.

But now she wasn't the only person I had.

Not only did Grandma visit me, but she wrote to me, and so did Mickey and Grandpa. Even Barry did. Sad letters telling me how sorry he was, and would I ever be his friend again. And I found I did still think of him as a friend. He was just a screwy kid, but no screwier than me.

So nearly every day I got a letter from someone. I got almost a whole book of drawings from Mickey. I even got a card from my dad. That I just tossed on the floor. Many of the kids there never got any letters, or ever had anyone visit them. I saw I was actually lucky, something I'd never thought before.

So I spent a lot of my sitting time writing letters back. Saying things I couldn't say out loud.

I also spent a lot of time reading, of course. But my favorites didn't work anymore. I found myself looking for books about people more like me, who had problems they couldn't solve just by shooting the bad guy.

And with all that writing and thinking and reading, the time went by. Driscoll had to admit I'd done a terrific job of sitting. By then it was spring. Grandpa was saying it was time to plow, and he could sure use my help.

So I got to go back to my grandparents' place, and back to Mickey. Except I was afraid I wouldn't be able to see her much. But Mickey had talked to her mom about that, and they'd talked to her dad, and to Grandma and Grandpa. I got the feeling just about everyone had been talking about me. Which wasn't the most comfortable feeling I've ever had.

But the result of all that talking was she came over the first day I was back. Next thing I knew she and I were walking out the gravel road, going up into the woods again. Something I'd imagined so many times during the past four months.

But it wasn't the way I'd imagined it.

In some ways it was better. I'd never been at my grandparents' place in the spring. I'd never seen it so green.

But I'd imagined me and Mickey together the way we'd been before. Instead, there was an arm's length or more between us, and neither of us seemed to know what to say.

Until we came to where the fire had been. Then Mickey's face lit up. "Yes!" she said. "I'd forgotten!"

How could she have forgotten the fire? And it didn't make my face light up.

"I want to show you something," she said. Then she frowned. "At least I think I have something to show you." She started toward where the old cabin had been.

I said, "Do we have to go there?"

But she wouldn't stop. And when we got to the clearing, right in the middle of that ugly mess of black and broken trees, there was this incredible patch of yellow. It was about six feet square. And solid yellow. I never knew flowers could grow so thick.

"They did it!" said Mickey

And it *was* amazing. I thought everything there had been killed.

"I think there's more than ever," she said. "Sometimes a fire will do that, kind of fertilize things."

Now that was a strange way to look at it. The fire had been *good* for the daffodils?

"I thought you'd like to see them," she said.

Yeah, or I never would've believed it could happen. And it wasn't just that they'd survived the fire. That cabin had been standing there empty—no telling how long—and those daffodils had just kept coming up?

Then Mickey said, "Are you mad at me?"

"Huh?" I turned to her. "Why would I be?"

"You're just so quiet. And you've been staying so far away from me."

"Me?" I thought she'd been the one keeping that distance between us.

"Is it because you talked to your mom?"

I said, "I haven't talked to my mom."

"Oh, I thought you had. Effie told me she called, yesterday. Guess she got the days mixed up. Anyway, when she found you weren't here yet, she said she'd call today. So I thought . . ."

Why would my mom want to talk to me now? I felt my insides twisting, changing. Here I'd been spending every minute of my time looking forward to being free, and now I felt like I was locked up again, being dragged somewhere I didn't want to go.

Mickey said, "Maybe I shouldn't have told you. I mean, the way your mom is, she'll probably forget, and not call again."

"That's for sure." But even as I said it, my voice sounding like I didn't care, the twisted mess that was now my insides told me it wasn't that simple. And I'd thought, what with all the thinking I'd been doing, that now I'd be able to forget my mom.

But I hadn't been able to forget her.

During those long nights at MacBride, I'd find myself crazily wondering if she would come to see me. Even wishing she would. Or I'd find myself worrying about how she was doing—thinking she had to be worried about me. And every time the mail came, I couldn't keep myself from looking first to see if her handwriting was on one of the envelopes.

And now I could feel part of me was actually glad she'd called. I even thought she might have changed, and I'd have a mom like you think moms are supposed to be. While the rest of me was ready to rip those daffodils up by the roots.

Guess whenever I'd told myself I was done with her, and I'd never again feel this anger burning up my brain—or this aching emptiness—that had been just another lie.

And I finally understood why my mom lied so much. It was something that had often puzzled me, since I couldn't see that it had ever really won her much of anything.

It was that some lies are a whole lot easier than the truth.

But I didn't want to ever give up again.

What I wanted to do was to make that space between me and Mickey go away. You could see that was what she wanted too. So why was it so hard for me?

But I took a good look at those daffodils. Until I'd gotten over the idea of ripping them out of the ground. Then I said, "You know, I've really missed you. Guess it's just going to take me a while." And I reached across that space.

'Cause I figured a person ought to be at least as strong as a flower.